Cullen B. Aubery

Twenty-Five Years on the Streets of Milwaukee after Dark

Cullen B. Aubery

Twenty-Five Years on the Streets of Milwaukee after Dark

ISBN/EAN: 9783744790048

Printed in Europe, USA, Canada, Australia, Japan

Cover: Foto ©Andreas Hilbeck / pixelio.de

More available books at **www.hansebooks.com**

TWENTY-FIVE YEARS

ON THE

STREETS OF MILWAUKEE

AFTER DARK;

TOGETHER

WITH SKETCHES OF EXPERIENCES AS NEWSBOY IN
THE ARMY, CAPTURE AND IMPRISONMENT
IN LIBBY PRISON, AND OTHER
WAR-TIME NOTES AND
INCIDENTS.

BY C. B. (DOC) AUBERY.

J. H. Yewdale & Sons Co., Printers and Engravers, Milwaukee, Wis.
1897.

1206

PREFACE.

On the very day when I confidently expected my book would be ready for delivery to 5,000 cash in advance subscribers and an anxiously waiting world for its appearance, with a new era of rejuvinated prosperity trotting along by its side, I met the printer who was charged with the great responsibility of producing it and he said to me:

"Doc, you haven't written a preface."

"By the Great Jehovah, and the Continental Congress," said I, "that's right. I'll do it."

As I crossed the street I met an old-time friend, who said he understood I was getting out a book to be filled with my hitherto unpublished experiences "On the Streets of Milwaukee After Dark, During Twenty-five Years," and asked what I was doing it for.

"Fifty cents in paper covers; $1 in cloth," said I, "with no discount victims."

He looked at me through his eyes fully a minute, then said: "Oh, that's altogether different. Here's a dollar; put me down for two."

This ought to reveal my purpose and put my friends on for falling in at the first roll call. Some matters of interest may be left untouched. Twenty-five years on the streets after dark have naturally revealed to me some things which even a special policeman don't care to touch too freely. But most of them will naturally suggest themselves to the skillful reader, as a wink is as good as a nod to a blind auctioneer. See?

"Facts are facts—
For he who dares think one thing and would another tell
My heart hateth like the gates of hell."

—"Doc."

OLD CHIEF'S GOOD ADVICE.

One day a friend said to me:

" 'Doc,' you've been out so much nights you must have seen a great many things of interest not reported in the newspapers."

"Yes," said I, "I've seen a great many things, but, to tell you the truth, my boy, they all look pretty much alike."

June 12, 1897, completed twenty-five years of service for me as special police officer, around a few blocks in the

"Don't Tell Everybody About It."

Wisconsin street business centre. That takes us back further than we can look ahead. It goes back to the days when there were no telephones, no police patrol wagons, no electric lights or electric cars, no lightning messengers with rusty jointed knees, no bicycles to make an excuse for every person on the street having a-leg-I-see most any hour, without even asking permission, and only a few of some other things which are quite numerous now. Neither did the newspaper reporters have a club room then, supplied with automatic incubators for hatching news, but they had to get out and hustle to get in a good night's work.

In those old days, William Beck was the chief of police, William Kendrick was first lieutenant, and the venerable Thomas Shaughnessy was second lieutenant. Kendrick has been gathered in in the closing round-up, but Beck and Shaughnessy are still fairly active. There were no sergeants or roundsmen then and only about fifty men on the force, in which there are now 321, of which 275 are patrolmen, the balance officers.

Lieut. Kendrick kept the books at the station, Shaughnessy had charge of the men and Beck did the detective work and directed the whole affair, with the help of his brother as special detective, when needed.

I first met Mr. Beck when I went to him with a letter from Manager Mills, of the Chapman store, for an order for a star, which I still have. Mr. Mills had hired me on a thirty days' probationary period as special officer to keep an eye on the store nights. The noted Wheeler robbery had taken place a short time before and some of the merchants on Wisconsin street had decided to employ a man who would try to keep things clean and attend to business. A system of time clocks was put in, at my suggestion, so there could be no mistake as to whether the watchman did his duty.

When Mr. Beck handed me the order for a star, he said:

"Now, my boy, you've got quite an important job to keep up there, and if you should see a cat go along the street with a dog's head on, don't go and tell everybody about it."

At the time I was not quite sure of just what he meant, but concluded it was a hint, to mind my own business. It was a hint worth two kicks. Push it along.

IMPORTANCE OF DRUG STORES.

I soon learned that the drug stores on a beat required special attention at the hands and feet of a night watchman, as, should there be a railroad accident or a big fire and someone hurt, a drug store was about the first place to be sought for remedies, and the night clerk, in his haste to get to bed, might have carelessly left a bottle of whisky right in the way where he would be pretty sure to fall over it in his hurry, just getting out of bed from a sound sleep, on an emergency call, and such things had to be looked after. Then, again, some duffer might·hold the clerk up, and if such a thing should happen, and the man on the beat did not know it, he'd be mighty thirsty the balance of the night. I believe I've never been accused of having failed to perform my full duty in connection with the drug stores on my beat.

"An Evil Spirit Shut the Door."

Fred Buckley was a clerk in Donnelly's drug store. One stinging cold night in January he got up to answer a call. When the customer had left he went out to the corner of the store to look up the alley at the North star. A draft of air or some evil spirit pushed the door shut, the spring lock sprung in with a snap and he was out for keeps, with his key in his vest pocket, inside. It was a still, sharp night, the mercury 22 below, and not a bird or a cat stirring. He had on only his shirt, trousers and slippers, and had to go two blocks to a hotel and wait while the night watchman went up to Twenty-third street and got the proprietor's key, so he could get in the store again. Of course Mike and I saw that he got back without being held up by footpads.

One Wehmer, who kept a drug store at the corner of Milwaukee and Mason streets, in the years that were, was a character. It made no difference who came to the store in the night, he would never dress, but come out in his "slumberette," and wait upon them. He was often to be seen wandering about the store in that costume in the night, which gave his place the name of "the ghost house." He had another characteristic, that of never drinking out of a cup. The night men on the street usually kept an eye to windward, to see that he didn't get held up in his ghostly attire. One afternoon we got a little vial of stuff from a clerk in another drug store and in the evening managed to dump it in a bottle in his back room, the contents of which he never drank out of a cup, and there was more than the usual activity in the ghost house that night.

There was another drug clerk whom it would be unfair not to mention. He still lives, is the husband of a handsome little woman and has a nice home, on the West Side. He had a reputation for making the best lemonade known to the natives or the night men either. One time a new man came on the beat. He had heard of the "illegant" lemonade my friend could make and had secreted in him a longing to sample it. It was a very hot night and about 11 o'clock we happened to meet at the right spot. I signalled the drug clerk for two lemonades which were taken care of in due time and nobody saw the croton oil bottle touched. The last half of that night was one of the most active ever put in by a new man on a beat. He made a solemn vow not to eat any more cucumbers and green corn that year.

TROUBLESOME CATS.

Streubig, the regular man on my beat, was a jolly, good-natured German, and the old women living in the neighborhood liked him because he would listen patiently to all of their complaints. One night an old lady living on the alley came out and asked Streubig to go in the back yard and chase the cats away so she could sleep. Streubig said he would and she went back to bed.

In about ten minutes the owner of the buildings came

along and in a confidential way said to me:

"See here, 'Doc.' you are around here all night. I have rented some rooms up in this building to young men for sleeping rooms. I think they need looking after, as one of my tenants has already told me she believed there was something wrong.

I said: "Oh, that's all right; them's cats. I know all about it, for an old lady living on the alley came out and

"That's All Right; Them's Cats."

asked Struebig to go around and drive the cats away so she could sleep."

He went away satisfied, and as Ed. Carey came along just then the conversation was turned in another direction and the "boys" had their time all right. You see it had been hinted to me that a beat kept clean, with no arrests upon it, and everybody satisfied was all that was required.

THE NEW POLICEMAN.

Then there was the new regular policeman. There is no place you can put a man where he will appear more awkward than during his first few nights on police duty.

It was a bitter cold night and the new man remarked that "a drop of the crathur would be a good thing, aven for a polaceman."

As I have often said, a drug store cut a figure on a beat. If the watchman and regular beat man don't see that the night clerk does not get held up, they may not get filled up. The new-made "cop" got it, but instead of rye it was Jamaica ginger. He thought it was a mistake and he had been poisoned.

"O! for the love of the Blissed Mary, sind for a praist," he cried, in burning words.

It was some time before we could convince him that it was only a part of the regular program and that he was merely stepping in the footprints of his illustrious predecessors.

After the fire had died out and we were on the beat again, I said to my friend:

"Mike, we'll get even with him."

"And may all the blissed Saints do be helpin' us to do thot same," said Mike.

And I reckon they did, for we got even.

It wasn't long until our friend, the drug clerk, had a night call to fill a prescription. As we merely happened along at the time, we obeyed the inward admonition to see that the clerk didn't get held up while the door was unbolted. As Mike remarked, it was a "boistorious night," early in March. By some means, during the filling of the prescription, an icicle as big as your arm and about a foot long got into the clerk's bunk. You wouldn't have begrudged two dollars to have heard him yell when he laid his spine on that icicle.

ABSENT-MINDED BANKER.

One of my first experiences in guarding business houses was an odd one. It was at the Old Insurance building, before it became "Old" by the building of the New

Insurance building.   At that time there was a bank in the
room on the ground floor now occupied by Des Forges'
book store.   It was a part of my duty to look after that
bank.   On my first round, one night, about 8 o'clock,
I found the front door open.   I went in and, to my utter
astonishment, the whole thing seemed to be running open.
Even the vault door was wide open.

"Holy Smoke! James Brothers, Younger Brothers,
and all the other Sunday school combinations," said I to
myself, "What in Heilen Blazes does all this mean?"   I

"What in Heilen Blazes Does All This Mean?"

looked under desks, in the stove, the cuspidors and all
other nooks and corners for burglars, but failed to find
them.   Then I went out on the sidewalk and looked
around.   The evening star, as well as my own, was in its
place, and the gas lights along the street were engaged in
their usual effort to get the legal requirement of seven
feet of gas an hour through five-foot burners.   Everything
seemed to be all right, except that cussed bank, which had
suddenly fallen into my sole-less possession, and I didn't
know what on earth to do with it.

Much to my relief, my friend Streeter, then with Hempsted's music store, across the street, came along. I knew him to be fully as honest as myself, and at once decided to take him into my confidence. I offered to divide the spoil with him even and proceed to loot the concern without further discussion or the adoption of any set resolutions. But he proved a disappointment. Whether he lacked nerve or ambition I never knew, but he flatly refused the offer and said:

"Tuerk lives in the next block to me and as I am just going home I will go over and tell him to come down and close the thing up for the day, or night."

In about three-quarters of an hour the boss of the bank hove in sight, coming leisurely down from the First ward. Coming up to me in an indifferent sort of way, he asked:

"'Doc,' what's matter?"

"Matter? Matter enough," said I. "Why, this thing is all open; even the coal bucket and the cot are open."

"There, by thunder," said he, feeling in his trowsers pocket, "I haven't got my key, now. It is lying on a shelf up at the house. I'll have to go back after it."

And what do you think he did? Sneaked back home and went to bed. I waited an hour for him; then got the regular officer on the beat to watch the place while I went after him, making my round of the other business houses as I went. After pounding my knuckles sore on his front door without getting a response I pulled a board off the fence and actually split the siding on his house pounding it to awaken him. But at last I got him out of bed, when he confessed that he had forgotten all about the bank when he got home. But he brought the key along that time, and after I saw the bank vault closed and the street door locked, fearing he might have forgotten the way home, I told him the way and went to hunt more burglaries. I afterwards learned what I had reason to suspect, that he was a very absent-minded man and had cut up some worse capers than that before, without any malice in 'em. Next day he placed a V in my hand and, with a sort of seven-be-nign, or, maybe, ten smile, said:

"Don't gimmeway."

AN EARLY TIME REPORTER.

One of the first acquaintances I made among newspaper men was Henry Bleyer, then a reporter on the Sentinel, where he has passed through many departments of the work of making a great newspaper, never leaving any yawning chasms in the position he held.   He was a regular hustler in those days and used to hunt me up, or down, regularly when he learned I was a regular knight of the

"Yes, There Were Two of 'Em."

beat, or beat of the night, for I thought I knew more about police duty than any man who had been "on the force" for years, as all new men do.   If Henry did not print all the important happenings on my beat, in the early days, some of the other fellows can thank his discretion or forgetfulness for it.   There were doubtless times when he regarded it as imprudent to disturb existing tranquility in some quiet neighborhoods.

One night, a little farther on in my experience, Henry thought he had sniffed a piece of sensational news. He came to me with his eyes on end and his hair sticking out and said:

"'Doc,' did you see anything a little suspicious along the street half an hour ago?"

"Yes," said I, "there were two of 'em; went towards the Northwestern depot; guess they took the 1 o'clock train for Chicago."

"I don't care to make trouble," said Henry, "but if I should catch him out that way, I think he'd take his meals down town a few days."

Then Henry went to the office and an hour later, when the two re-appeared I gave him a tip and got one in return.

A LIVELY TIME WITH GUNS.

One winter several young bloods occupied a suite of rooms in the vicinity of 401 Milwaukee street. They frequently had the company of several others of their set for an evening and occasionally there would be an hour or so during which dullness and inertia were as much strangers to their rooms as dyspepsia is to a dog. It was my custom to visit them occasionally, until I became satisfied their amusement was of the innocent kind which meant no harm to any one.

One night the gang trailed up the stairs and I knew by the indications that there was fun ahead.

In about fifteen minutes the fun began, and there was a lively popping of revolvers for a few seconds. The shooting quickly attracted a crowd on the street and people stood in fear, expecting a horrible murder was being or had been committed. Seeing the crowd was determined an investigation should be made, I insisted that the shooting was up a flight of stairs in the next building. The firing had ceased, the boys apparently realizing the noise would attract attention, but none of the spectators seemed anxious to go up in the dark and investigate.

Finally I went up—the wrong stairs, of course—looked around, came back and said:

"O, that's another case of cats. Fellow up there in a room shooting out of the back window at cats in the yard. Told him if I heard any more of it I'd run 'im in."

Then the crowd left and after a little I went up to see

"Another Case of Cats."

what the boys had been doing. They were sitting around a table taking care of a basket of champagne. They had placed a silk hat on each of the four bedstead posts and the one of four who got the smallest number of holes through a hat with six shots fired as rapidly as they could be fired, had to pay for the champagne. Hence the twenty-four revolver shots had been fired in the space of a very few seconds. The game had come painfully near being a tie, six bullets having went through each of three of the hats and five through the other one.

The silk hats were pretty badly cut up, but the Champagne was fine.

A FAMOUS SPRING.

When the excavation was made for the basement of a large building only a block from the corner of Wisconsin and Milwaukee streets, a big spring was tapped. It yielded a bounteous supply of water, which seemed as clear as crystal. The manager of the concern had it walled up with choice bricks and regarded it as a highly valuable find. The surplus water, that not drank by the people about the building, was trailed into the sewer. When the building came to be occupied the water from the spring was carried all through it in jugs and was drank in preference to hydrant water.

At the time George Peck and his Sun were at the zenith of their glory gained, and Peck's Sun was quoted in a majority of the newspapers throughout the country,

"Big Money in It for You."

both daily and weekly. One day the author of more than one "Bad Boy" at that time went into the office of the manager of the building and the chief business in it and said to the manager:

"I've an idea which may interest you."

"Yes, you seem to have several every week which interest a good many people," was the reply.

"Well, that may be, but this is a new one and there may be big money in it for you," said the "Bad Boys'" author.

That suggestion cut off all attempts at jesting on the part of the manager. He was all attention and invited the prospective governor to let his idea escape from its hiding place.

"I have been thinking about that spring of yours, down in the cellar," said Mr. Peck, "and am pretty thoroughly

impressed with the belief that it is worth more than all
of the religious printing establishments in the city, with
The Sentinel thrown in for wide margins. I have discovered a peculiar taste in the water, after it stands awhile,
and am inclined to believe it possesses rare medicinal
qualities. If I were in your place I wouldn't let any more
of that water go to waste. I would save it, bottle it, label
it "Ponce de Leon Spring Water," advertise it as from
the spring of eternal youth for which Old Ponce de Leon
sought, and make a fortune out of it."

That idea and suggestion had a decidedly active effect
upon the dignified manager. He rushed down into the
basement, hatless and coatless, knelt down at the spring
and took a long smell of it. Then he tasted it, smelled it
again and tasted it some more. The investigation satisfied
him that Mr. Peck was right and he decided to act at once
to save the water, of which there was a good two inch
stream running into the sewer, as there is yet. He sent a
messenger in haste to a big cooperage factory with an order
for 100 new oak whisky barrels, to be delivered instantly,
and another with a supplementary order for another 100
to be delivered on call. The entire force of employes was
set to barreling water, special men were hired to continue
the work, and the night watchman instructed to guard
it carefully. The manager sat up nearly all night design-
ing a bottle and label for the water and had an artist
drawing a picture of Ponce de Leon for the label.

Peck's Sun went to press next day and quite early in
the morning Mr. Peck called again to see if the manager
wouldn't like a preliminary "ad." of the spring in The
Sun. That suggestion was as promptly accepted as the
other had been and, together the heads of two great newspapers set out to write the "ad." While at work on the
"ad.," Mr. Peck suggested that they ought to have an
analysis of the water in order to made the announcement
a clincher. It was decided to get an analysis as quickly
as possible, but it couldn't be had in time for that issue
of the Sun, so Mr. Peck suggested a column of a general
and glowing write-up of the spring, at $1 a line, with a
promise of an analysis the next week. As The Sun then
had over 100,000 circulation, covering the whole coun-

try, of course $1 a line was cheap, and the column grew into nearly two coulmns, but the article was too good to be cut, and it all went. If I remember correctly Mr. Peck told me his bill was a little under or a little over $300, and was paid the next day.

Some of the water was taken to a chemist with orders to rush out an analysis of it regardless of cost, and the process of barreling the products of the spring went on while a large order was placed for bottles and a fine label engraving started.

In a few days the chemist sent word that if they would take the trouble to trace that vein of water back a few hundred feet they would be dead sure to find it running right through the vault of some old outhouse. That ended the spring fortune and the next issue of Peck's Sun contained a humorous apology for the non-appearance of the analysis of the famous water, there was a big lot of new white oak barrels for sale at a discount, and a countermand of orders for bottles and labels was issued.

IN A DISSECTING ROOM.

Though the Cosmopolitan restaurant was a thing of but a brief period, it lived long enough to have at least one sensation developed in its immediate vicinity. The first intimation I had of the affair was about two o'clock on the morning before it was made public. At that time I saw a horse and buggy with three men in it go up Wisconsin street at a pretty lively gait, and turn north on Jefferson. A sort of graveyard feeling that everything wasn't quite right crept over me and I hustled up to the corner and looked north, but the buggy had disappeared. Half an hour later the same rig came off Milwaukee street and went down Wisconsin street at about a 2:10 gait, with only two men in the buggy. Suspicion No. 2 got into my think tank then and I would have bet a drink with any drug clerk on the beat that something was off color somewhere. I kept a close eye on ground floors on my beat the balance of the night, but without discovery.

It was two o'clock next morning when Jim Meba Nahn, one of the smoothest reporters of those days, said to me:

"'Doc,' did you know there was a 'stiff' on your beat?"

"What? Who's dead?" said I.

"No, not that," said he, "but the doctors have got a subject and are hacking it up."

"Hellendam nation! is that so? Where?" said I.

"Alone With a Supposed Corpse."

"You read the morning paper and you'll get on," said he.

My discoveries of twenty-four hours previous were still in my think box and this was enough. I knew there was but one place on my beat where the thing would likely be, and I made a stroll. With my Vermont Yankee guesser at work I struck it the first time.

I went down a back basement stairs, lit my bullseye lantern, turned the knob of the door, which was not even locked, and stepped inside. "Jimminy crack," said I to myself, "this is dead easy, unless Dr. Brow Han is here and catches me at it." I listened. All was still. Then I turned the cap of the bullseye, looked around and began exploring. There wasn't a sign of life, or of death, either, in sight; but I kept up the search. Around in an obscure corner of the basement was an old table and upon it a bunch of something covered with an old white cloth. It looked a little spookish, but I lifted up the cloth and there it was, the body of a man, the head and one arm cut off and missing.

The sight reminded me of the first Johnny Reb. I saw hit by a shell at Bull Run. I looked the cadaver over carefully, but there were no visible marks by which it could be identified. Then I left, taking a precaution, which the owner had not, to loose the spring lock on the basement door.

The morning paper had the story under a big head— not the missing head of the cadaver—of a medical college dissecting room in a basement within a stone's throw of the postoffice.

Next night, as I was going on duty, Douglass Flint, the proprietor of the Cosmopolitan, a good natured, fat, congenial chap who, later, joined an opera troupe, and is still with it, singing bass, was standing on his front step and accosted me with:

"See here, 'Doc,' come in here and go down in my basement and, bygawd, sir, you'll find there is no medical college in there."

"Keep still," said I; "that's all right. You keep quiet, put a few of your friends on and after you close up, I'll show you where it is."

Then I went and tipped off a scheme to a drug clerk. After closing time he and I went in the back room, took a piece of board and smeared upon it a horribly distorted face of a man, leaving bear streaks and spots to represent eyes, mouth, numerous cuts and slashes, etc. We used phosphorus paste to paint the thing. Phosphorus, you know, shines in the dark, but makes no show in the light. Then we turned out the light. The thing was a corker. The drug clerk almost fainted at the sight. After taking an unusually large section of precaution against the possibility of the clerk being held up later on, I took the board and planted it in the right spot in a ghostly dingy unoccupied basement in the vicinity, that had enough dark alleys and passageways in it to make it a terror, even in the daytime, unless one had a light and a guide. There were two entrances to the basement and I fixed both just right, so the spring locks would work well.

The Cosmopolitan man had a set of his friends ready in his back room and pretty well "braced" for the occasion. I will not name them, as a number of them are still here in business and have interesting families.

About two o'clock a. m. I tickled the front door latch and was admitted. The proprietor provided a round of precautionary nerve supporter and I led the way out the back door, the four invited guests to the feast following in silence. Into the basement, as dark as darkest Egypt, we went and closed the door, the spring lock doing its duty. Then I lit a stub of a candle and led them through three or four crooked passageways, enough to aid them in losing their bearings, and back into a corner not far from the side entrance. Of course the body had been removed during the early part of the night, so there was no danger of them falling over it. I cautioned them to keep still, saw, by a glance, that my board was all right. Then my light went out and I slipped out through the side door, closing it, let the spring lock on and slid up onto the street. The sight hunters were alone in the basement, with a supposed corpse and a phosphorus visage staring them in the face. Not until one of them stumbled against the phosphorescent board and found what it was, did they realize that they had been sold. I proceeded to look after my beat. One of the party happened to have matches in his pocket and in about an hour they found a way out. To this day they will all swear that the newspaper story about a corpse being hacked up in a basement was a base lie.

I am quite sure, however, that the framework of the object of their search, properly mounted, can be seen in one of Mr. Nehrling's glass cases in the Public Museum. It went there as a present from Dr. Brow Han.

A MINE SPECULATOR'S JAMBOREE.

Some years ago a fellow who had made quite a lot of money in mine speculations, and has since figured as chief attraction in a big failure, decided to celebrate his success by giving a banquet to his friends. He had third floor rooms on Milwaukee street in which he decided to bring out the affair. At that time the Cosmopolitan restaurant was in full blast and regarded as

"Mr. 'Doc,' Dey Beats de Berry Debil."

a first class caterer for well up affairs, and this affair was to be well up—two long flights. A big spread was laid. Champagne flowed like water in a brook or gore in a slaughter house. There was orchestral music and the dulcet notes of the cats in the neighborhood were temporarily snowed under.

The moon had retired from view, the flickering flames in the gas lamps were beginning to take on a sort of tired, pale hue. The measured step of the regular man on the beat grew fainter. In the semi-silence of the hour when skilled housebreakers grow active, the popping of champagne bottle corks was move distinctly heard.

Suddenly, after a few minutes of comparative stillness in that upper region, there came a crash. It sounded like all of the glass roof-lights in the town were coming down. It was a racket to awaken the dead. Down the stairs came dishes, chinaware, bottles, chairs, colored waiters, tubs of water and chopped ice, tin buckets and things almost innumerable. Colored waiters, furniture and broken crockery came rolling down those two flights of stairs in startling confusion.

The regular man on the beat was four blocks off and I was three. We both ran for the scene of the sounds, expecting to find a building collapsed. I got there first and just as the three colored waiters were picking themselves up and sorting their individual personages out of the wreck.

"What's matter?" said I.

"Lawdy! Moses! Mr. 'Doc', Dey beats de bery debil!" said one of them. "Dey's got done eatin' an' drinkin' an' is jes' cleanin' up de room. Golly! but its a long ways down dem sta'rs. Dis niggah's gwine home."

And the waiters hurried off, rubbing their shins and picking pieces of broken crockery out of their wool.

"Be jabbers, Oi was foor blocks aff, but Oi do be thinkin' thim laddiebucks must be about six," said Mike, as he looked at the wreckage.

The fact was, the banquet was finished, part of the guests had departed and in order to get things out of the way so the balance, the host and his intimate chums could spread out cots and have a snooze, they had thrown everything not needed down stairs in a bunch. Mike and I awoke the proprietor of the Cosmopolitan and helped him clean up about seven bushel basketfulls of the wreckage before daylight. Next day the host cashed up in full and wisely fenced all knowledge of the affair in from the daily papers. He wanted a time, had it and didn't care what it cost.

TWO IN TROUBLE.

An incident occurred on my beat one night. It was a night in January, with the thermometer registering 20 below and about the hour when graveyards are supposed to yawn and ghosts stalk forth. A young man rooming near the postoffice came running down the street with apparently only his shirt, trowsers and slippers on. Whatever else he may have had on earlier had been disposed of. He made a straight rush for a drug store. So did I. I had seen earlier and took in the situation at

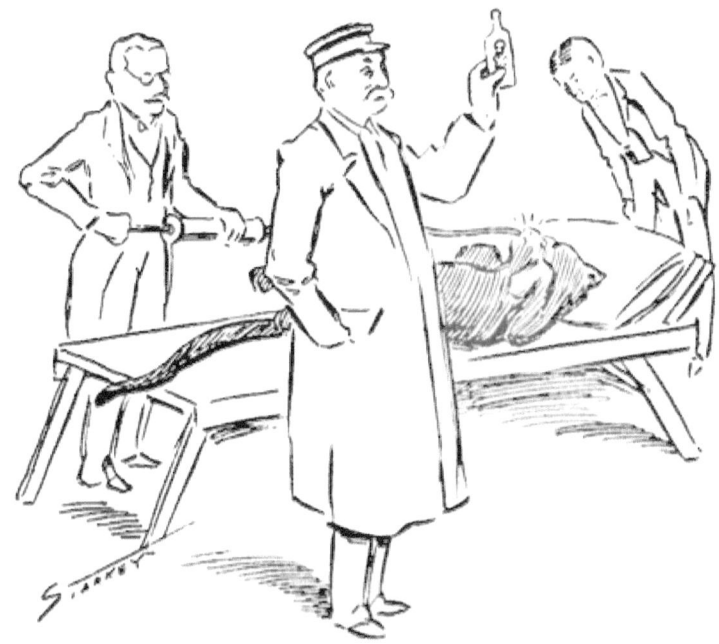

"She's All Right. That's Not the First Time."

a glance. I came up as he was pushing the night clerk's bell and asked: "What's matter?"

Still pushing the bell he said: "'Doc', where can I get a doctor? Man has taken poison in my room."

My first impression was that it was another case of cats. However, I said: "Go back and I'll fetch a doctor."

I got a doctor and we started for the room in a hurry. The doctor took along an instrument which looked like a miniature pile driver and went to work, like a fire boat, pumping 'er out. I found on the floor a bottle labeled "laudanum" and, after due observation, went my way to look for more burglars, or cats, or other people in trouble, leaving the doctor working like a night scavenger.

In about an hour the doctor came down and I asked him: "How is *he* getting along?"

"She's all right," said he. "That's not the first time. I've done that before. It is a case of membretious."

The fellow at he drug store, whom I will call Goerge, and who sold the laudanum, was badly scared when shown the bottle and told that she had taken all of its contents.

"If she has she is dead, sure," said he. But she wasn't, though she is now.

A BATH IN PASTE.

Did you ever fall into a paste mine? If not you don't know what fun is, real good, sticky fun—for everybody who catches you at it. At least that was my experience, and I had some. One evening, just at quitting-work time, an expressman left a barrel of flour paste at the top of the entrance to the basement of the Evening Wisconsin building. The hands all escaped without taking it down into the mailing room, where it belonged.

Just after dark some Third ward arabs ran against the barrel, stopped, investigated and held a council of war. Then they sent out skirmish lines and soon had reports in to the effect that "dere was no 'cop' around." Then they massed their forces and dumped the barrel down the stairs, end over end. As the barrel ended over onto the second step down, the lower head succumbed to the pressure and out went the paste with a slush and flooded over the steps, like an onion poultice on a fried beefsteak. With a yell of triumph the kids vanished into the Third ward darkness, doubtless mentally calculating on the extent of that piece of deviltry and speculating on where their next opportunity would develop.

With the regularity of an Elgin time-piece I went the rounds of my beat. The darkness around the stairway was about as thick as the paste on the steps, but, gazing intently into that fateful pit I became satisfied there was

"Thought I Must be a Sight."

an object at the bottom which seemed to lie quiet, like a crockodile in a Louisiana stream. I got my war courage together and started to descend the stairs.

As my left foot touched the second step it shot out from under me, like a boat going down the shoots, and my whole anatomy came after in a bunch. Ker thump, thump, thump I went down to the bottom, the swell of my pants dismally disfiguring the placid countenance of that paste on the steps, and I was right in it at the bottom of the pit.

I tried to get out, but it was useless. Every time I'd crawl up one step I seemed to slide back two. The stairway was paste everywhere and so was I. Just as despair, like a dismal ghost, was beginning to take possession of me and the pit of paste, George Hansen, then the regular policeman on the beat, came along and pulled me out. Since my escape from Libby prison, in 1862, I had never been so glad to get out of anywhere.

I thought I must be a sight. George thought so too, and proceeded to emphasize his thoughts with comments and a degree of hilarity totally devoid of anything bordering on sympathy. There was paste in my shoes, up my trowsers legs, in my pockets and even in my hair. I was decorated from head to foot with the slimy stuff and will never forget the look John Black gave me as I met him a few minutes later at the Chapman store corner. Nor will I forget the reception a neighboring druggist gave me when I went in his back room to clean up. He was a cold-blooded sort of fellow, who couldn't appreciate fun, anyway.

But the meanest part of the whole transaction was that after the many ways in which I had befriended Hansen, he should go and peddle the story broadcast, and among people who could neither appreciate real fun nor sympathize with an unfortunate. Yes, sir; Hansen peddled and paraded that story during fully a week, to the utter neglect of all other jokes and scandals, even after I had requested him to keep mum.

But I resolved and affirmed, by the sacred snout of the holy hippopotamus, to get even with Hansen. And I didn't have to wait long for an opportunity. It wasn't more than a week before Hansen complained to me, one morning that he was suffering terribly from piles. There was my opportunity and I inwardly chuckled with fiendish glee, as I looked up Wisconsin street at the rising sun.

"That so, George?" I asked. "Why didn't you tell me before? I've suffered many a barrel full with that infernal trouble; walked my beat many a night when it seemed as though I couldn't crawl around. But I found a remedy at last that fixed it right off. I've got no fear of piles now. One application does the business every time."

He begged to know what it was and I earnestly informed him that it required but one application of spirits of turpentine to completely cure that sort of human ailment. In proof of my sincerity I gave him a two ounce vial of it that I had in my pocket which I carried with me against a possible time of need.

George thanked me profusely and after receiving instructions as to how to use the remedy went home. Another man walked his beat several nights and when George came back he was cured—of telling the story of 'Doc' and the paste. I didn't expect he'd ever forgive me, but I guess he did, for he never after mentioned his application or the treatment, and a month later, when I was going away for a week, to attend an Iron Brigade reunion he came along and said: "Here, 'Doc,' is a present for you." And he handed me a nice cane with a big silver head and my name engraved upon it. I have it yet and prize it highly, but never look at it without thinking of the time I had with that blasted paste.

SOME WILD ANIMALS.

In the heart of a great city isn't a natural place to go hunting wild game. Yet, in my time on the streets quite a bag of it has been taken within a block of the postoffice. I can count up six skunks, two coons, a porcupine, a mud hen, a duck, a big mud turtle, and a mink.

Where the Windsor hotel now stands was a vacant lot with some piles of stones and old boards and a barn upon it. A colony of skunks had possession of the property. Almost every night one old fellow could be seen going up the postoffice alley on a foraging expedition to the garbage box back of Conroy's. As there was no immediate danger of him holding up a drug clerk I judiciously concluded that the alley belonged to that skunk at that particular hour of night. But one night I let a rock drop on him just as he was approaching the hole under the fence, through which he was accustomed to crawl back into the vacant lot. I didn't remain to argue matters, but all next day people seemed to prefer the other side of the street.

Dr. Hatchard afterwards killed one of the lot in his

stairway and did not do any considerable office business
for several succeeding days. It was most as bad a stink,
in some respects, as he got into before his family moved
north.

When the Tabor house was in existence, on Milwaukee street, one of the skunks was on the street near the
hotel. Dan Daggett, an old time citizen who lived there,
came home a little off color, as usual, saw the varmint,
thought it was a cat and gave it a kick. Moley Hoses!

"Howly Murther! The Divil Take Yez!"

Well, he didn't sleep that night. That was a case of cat,
for sure.

Early one morning I discovered a porcupine under a
cross walk opposite the postoffice. A driver of a mail
wagon said: "Wait till I get my dog." He had one
of those open countenanced, undershot bull dogs,
brought him out to the walk and said, "Sic 'im Tige."

Mr. Tige went under that walk with an energy worthy
a better occasion, but, Gee Whiz, you ought to have
seen his nose when he retreated.

We dispatched the varmint and left it lie by the gas
post, when along came John Dolan, a Third ward con-
tractor. I said: "John, did you ever see such a bird
as that?" He grabbed it, but as promptly let go and
howled:

"Howly murther! The divil take yez!" Then he began picking quills out of his hands. I ventured the suggestion that I did not tell him to pick it up, which only had the effect of doubling his volume of cuss words.

"Howly St. Patrick! I'll have to go to Dr. Wolkitt," said John, and he went off swearing and picking his hands while everybody else in sight laughed till John's oaths were smothered, like the bleat of a stray lamb in a March gale.

Tom Fiskin, the lamp lighter, and I caught the mud hen under the same crossing and I now have it mounted as one of the trophies of my experiences on the streets after dark.

The duck was evidently a lost in a fog victim. One night, when the fog was so thick I had to work through it edgewise in order to get through at all, the duck fell at my feet in the postoffice alley after flying against a telegraph wire. The bird's misfortune gave me duck for dinner next day, and didn't enrich Charley Higgins a quarter or two.

It was back during the Greely-Grant campaign that Mike, the regular man on the beat, and I caught two coons on the lot where Charley Pfister's tavern now stands. Whether they came in on some lumber vessel from up the lake, or had been brought by some Republican enthusiast to use in a celebrating procession after election, we never knew. We ran them up a tree that stood on the lot, Mike borrowed a dog and a pole, down in the Third ward. We pushed the coons off the limb with the pole, the dog did the balance, and Mike presented them to the Irishwoman who owned the dog.

One evening in the spring of '75 I found a big mud turtle in an alley back of Chapman's store. He flourished for a time in the Court house park fountain and was then transferred to a soup kettle in a down town restaurant.

It is only four or five years ago that I discovered a mink darting under a crossing opposite the postoffice. It wasn't five minutes before there were half a dozen men chasing that poor little defenseless mink, as he darted from one crossing and hiding place to another. Walter

Ellis was among the rush and he came nearest getting the game by trying to fall upon it just as the little brat went into a hole under a building. That was the last seen of the mink, but Ellis, in his fall, bursted the knee of a pair of $6 trousers, broke a suspend, tore out a buttonhole in his collar and got a pair of clean cuffs ready for the laundry.

The last skunk killin' around the postoffice was of recent date. It occurred only a few months ago, at the south basement entrance and was made the subject of big headlines and long articles in the daily papers. Half a dozen persons and half as many revolvers figured in the dispatching of the "critter," and the after effect was noticeable several days. Democrats around the government building tried to charge the odor to another Republican getting a place in the building. Republicans claimed another Democrat had just moved out and the apartments were being cleaned up. Thus the sparring went on while the odor lasted. The smell was certainly bounteous. It wouldn't have made a bad disinfectant for city civil service headquarters in the city hall.

That afternoon I met Postmaster Porth on the postoffice steps and he said:

" 'Doc,' what the devil was you doin' 'round here this morning to stir up such a smell?"

I replied: "O, that wasn't me; that was Win Nowell trying to drive you out."

He took a few sniffs of the air, still fragrant with the smells of the morning, and replied:

"No; this isn't so bad as that would be."

Captain O'Connor, superintendent of letter carriers, insisted that the smell reminded him of a poem written by a St. Louis girl, many years ago, when the city was very dirty. He said the poem was published in the Globe-Democrat and created a sensation. The first verse ran:

"Go see what I have sawn;
Go feel what I have felt;
Go out at early dawn
And smell what I have smelt."

The Captain said there were 763 more verses of the

poem and he was preparing to rehearse the whole lot at the house-warming in the new Federal building when it was ready to occupy.

Quite likely that was the last skunk killing that will be witnessed around the old Federal building. It is rumored that Judge Jenkins may put up one of his famous injunctions against their coming. If that wouldn't stop the skunks, it would likely outrival the after effects of their visit.

A CASE OF JIMS.

Away back in the old, old times, a year before the present unfinished new federal building was begun, after the properties it now occupies had been condemned by the government and most of the buildings moved off or torn down, there was an old barn standing near the centre of the block and an incident occurred in it one night.

As the entire property was unoccupied, not much trouble was gone to in the matter of lighting it and it was about as dismal a locality in the middle of a night as one could find in the heart of the city. The regular officer on the beat and I happened to meet about one a. m. on the sidewalk just east of the Milwaukee Club and opposite the dilapidated property. Suddenly we were startled by fearful screams in the old barn. They indicated that some poor fellow was being murdered. He was begging piteously for his life.

We both started on a run for the old barn. There was but one door to the barn that was open. We reached it together and jumped inside, the regular officer shouting:

"Let up, there, you villain!"

Inside the barn was as dark as a negro dance in a charcoal pit and we stopped just inside the door expecting a would-be murderer to try to escape and we would be in position to bag him. Apparently no heed was taken to the officer's command, as the poor victim kept on screaming and begging for his life.

"Get outside and light your bug," said the officer.

personal safety seeming enjoin against striking a match inside to reveal our location to a murderer who might have an arsenal attached to him.

I slipped outside and around a corner of the barn, scratched a match and lit my bullseye, the pleading still being kept up. I turned the dark slide over the bullseye and jumped into the barn again by the officer's side. Together we felt our way to within a few feet of the place where the tragedy seemed to be taking place, the bullseye in my left hand and each of us with a revolver in our right hand.

By a touch of his left hand the officer gave me the signal to halt and turn on the light. I pushed back the slide and let light onto the scene.

The barn floor was not flooded with human gore and there was no sign of a murderer there. There was just one poor fellow, in his shirt sleeves, bare-headed, sawing the air with his arms and defending himself against an imaginary murderer.

At the sight of the light he ran into a corner, let out an unearthly yell and stood trembling with fear. The policeman merely said:

"Jims," and our revolvers went into our pockets, and the officer pulled out his "bracelets." The fellow fought like a hyena, but we downed him by main force, without hurting him and tied his hands with a click. Then he began kicking. While the officer held him I found a piece of twine off a bale of hay and we tied his feet. Then we carried him out to the corner and called for the patrol wagon, realizing that it would be useless to take him to his home, though it was but a couple of blocks away. In about six weeks he came home from a Keeley Cure institution and I never heard of him drinking a drop since. He is prosperous in business in a Northern Wisconsin town now.

A CAMPAIGN INCIDENT.

It was just at the rear end of the Tilden and Hendricks campaign. The Democrats had a big organization called the Tilden and Hendricks guard. It had been out for a long parade in the evening and some of the more conspicuous leaders had enjoyed a vigorous piece of the juicy aftermath, which often tags in behind such an occasion, for the purpose of planning the distribution of the offices which are to be their's after the battle is ended and won.   Charley —— of the Seventh Ward was an officer in the tramping column and had evidently become pretty weary, as a result of one part or the other of the night's program.

The old Miner residence, which occupied the present

"What Devil Ye Doin' Here, Charley?"

site of the Pfister hotel and afterwards served as headquarters for several political parties and organizations, was then standing and the alley running through the block at the west side of the hotel ran close to it.   About 5 o'clock in the morning I looked up the alley and saw a dark object handing on the fence, on the alley side.   I walked up and there was Charley, his breast bone balanced on the fence, his shoulders, arms and head hanging over, and he was sleeping and snoring as soundly as a whole graveyard.

It was apparent that some other persons had discovered him before me and perpetrated a mean joke on him. They had unbuttoned his suspenders, both front and back and let his trowsers drop down around his feet. There he hung and slept, his bare legs and as much more of him as was unprotected by his "seemore" coat, a hapless victim to the frosty morning air.

My first impulse was to get a piece of board and arouse him by an application of it to his back settlements, but a lingering spark of humanity and fellow feeling in me got the better of the thought and I gave him a slap on the shoulder and said:

"What devil ye doin' here, Charley?"

He partially straightened up and replied:

"B'n out havin' lot fun 'ith Shtilden 'n' Henr'ks guard. 'T's helva time. Ain't I a daisy b'gosh?"

"You may be a daisy, but you don't wear the odor of one," said I. "Come on here; dress yourself and I'll take ye home."

He was wonderfully and fearfully loaded. I helped him get fixed up and took him to his home, only a couple of blocks away. I never meet him now but he asks:

"'Doc,' how's the Tilden and Hendricks Club?"

My answer is: "Owl right, Charley; I saw you up and dressed." Then he says:

> "'O, memory.
> Thou art a volume rich in sacred love.'"

And he moves on whistling: "How dear to my heart are the scenes of my childhood."

PAT AND THE PUSH CART.

Pat Howe was an old time policeman. The Third ward was his beat and it gave him his hands full. One hot summer morning about two o'clock, Pat came up Milwaukee street with a push cart and a load on it which made him puff like a fire tug to keep the wheels rolling. As he came up to the Chapman store corner, he seemed pretty well exhausted. It was before the days of telephones or patrol wagons, and a policeman had to get his pickups to the station as best he could, and that night Pat had taken in his hands full.

"Hello, Pat," said I, "what'smatter? Peddlin' bananas? What ye goin' to do with it?"

"Hey, 'Doc'," said he, "for the love of the Saints, come 'n' gimme a lift, plase; Oi'm toired out intoirely, so Oi am."

Pat had a big Irish woman in the cart. He found her on the street stone drunk and it was his imperative duty to take her to the station. The push cart was the only available vehicle and he was laboring hard with the load and having plenty of trouble to keep the woman's legs from getting tangled in the wheels.

"Well, now, Pat," said I, "I'm a little particular about

"What Ye Goin' to do with It?"

what sort of a job I undertake. I don't fancy that one very heartily."

"Sure, Mr. Aubery," said he, "Oi've pushed this d—' cart and carcass from beyant Detrite strate, and by me soul Oi'm about played out. It 'ud be a great favor if ye'd guv me a lift over til thu station wid it."

Realizing that I was only a sort of fifth wheel to the official wagon, anyway and Pat being the best kind of a good fellow, I fell in and helped him to the station.

About the time we reached the station the woman began to come to her senses, and as the man on duty there helped us lift her out and get her on her pins she real-

ized where she was. Then she turned on Pat and such
a tongue lashing as she gave him. She declared he was
no gentleman and his mother before him was no gentleman and called him all sorts of things for taking a
"dacint, respictable lady" to the station at that hour of
night.

Both she and Pat have been a long time dead. Pat
often said that was the hardest job he ever struck while
on the "force."

AN IMPORTED REPORTER.

As a rule newspaper reporters have always stood well
with the night watchmen. There has been a sort of
reciprocity existing between them which has seldom
been violated. As a rule, if we give a reporter an item
and say, "don'tgimme'way," the request has been relig-
iously regarded. Few nights have passed in the last
twenty-five years that reporters haven't come to me to
see if I had a tip on an item of news, and there are few
of them who will accuse me of having failed to try to
help them out.

One night, soon after the assassination of President
Garfield, one came to me and said:

"'Doc,' I want an item mighty badly; it is a desper-
ately dull night."

I tapped on my think tank and remarked that we'd
have to get an item, then. Said I:

"There's a pair of old trousers down the alley; there's
an old coat over yonder on a basement stairs, an old
hat in an ash box up on Milwaukee street and a lot of
straw in a crockery crate a little further on. D'ye see?"

"Owl right," said he.

Next morning an effigy of Guiteau was hanging to
the limb of a tree near the Milwaukee Club, and the
morning paper had an item of news.

When the Republican and News was in its clovery
days, an imported reporter was brought in from Canada
to show the home boys how it ought to be done. He
was a hummer. He would hunt me up, or down, every
hour in the night to see if I'd caught a burglar or any

cats, or cadavers, etc. It was he who reported, in half a column, a man having hanged himself to a gooseberry bush in Wauwatosa. He took somebody's word for it.

One night he discovered a fire and got the fire department out. He had met me at Milwaukee and Mason streets and was discussing the scarcity of news, when, suddenly, the light of the blast furnaces at the rolling mills loomed up in fine style. It was the first time he had seen that light and he was sure it was a big fire on the south side.

With one wild whoop he flew away towards fire department headquarters. It was worth a quarter, at least, just to see his coat-tails fan him along down the street. In less than a minute the department was on the street and racing down Broadway. That was the last time he ever went to the Boardway engine house. The boys swore if he ever came around there again they would tie loose the hose on him. He was too swift for this town and the paper soon exported him back to Canada. He'd shown the home boys how to do it.

ONE OF HARRY SUTTER'S JOKES.

Fritz Callis was the pioneer saloon keeper at the Academy of Music, and he was something of a character. Once he got a barrel of new cider and put it in his back room. In a few days it got to working. It was a barrel which had some experience before and the faucet hole in the head was plugged with a cork. When the cider got well to working it began to sing. Fritz discovered it and called me in to see what was the matter of it. I told him I guessed it was alive.

"Yah, I think me so couple times already once," said Fritz. "But vhat I petter done mit him?"

I suggested that he take a hatchet and tap it gently on the head around the corked hole. He did it and zip went the cork to the ceiling and a stream of cider followed it.

"Mine Gott!" said Fritz, "dot thing he drown me my house out."

"Stick your thumb in the hole, Fritz," said I, "and stop it."

Into the hole went Fritz's thumb and by pushing down hard he could stop the flow. I told him I would go to a neighboring saloon and get a wooden faucet to drive in, so he could draw out enough to ease the pressure on the barrel.

A couple of blocks away I met the regular officer, a fun-loving Irishman, and told him the snap I had gotten Fritz into. He went down and consoled Fritz about an

When Charley Kraus Discovered the Bomb.

hour, when I returned, of course, unable to find a faucet. We kept him at the hole half an hour longer, suggesting various ways for his release, then I whittled a pine tap and plugged the barrel. Fritz always declared that hugging a cider barrel an hour and a half was no joke, yet he had a suspicion that I didn't make very great haste to release him.

After a while Charley Kraus opened a saloon two doors north from Fritz's and it nearly broke Fritz's heart. Charley was a sound Republican, a jolly good fellow and his place promptly became prominent with the boys. He could beat the world on a clam bake and that won him high favor with the Whist Club members. There was a photographer in town by the name of Harry Sutter, who would rather perpetrate a joke on a fellow mortal than photograph a whole family of babies at a dollar and a half apiece. He was a frequent caller at Charley's place and usually took a friend or two with him.

One night business was slow and Charley had fallen asleep in his chair. The photographer was ready for business and had been watching for an opportunity several days. That was his time. He had a piece of gas pipe about nine inches long with the ends corked and a piece of wool twine in one end. He lighted the twine, slipped in on tip toe, laid the pipe under Charley's chair and escaped. As he reached the sidewalk he let out a whoop which awoke the sleeper. Charley smelled burning twine, looked down and saw the bomb under his chair.

Wild with fright, he fairly flew from the place, ran to the nearest corner and told those attracted by his strange actions that some one had thrown a bomb in his place and the whole thing would be blown to smithereens in about a minute. The photographer led the crowd back to the saloon, picked up the gas pipe and threw it into the street. Quite a crowd had gathered and all took what they liked—on Charley.

GARNER MURDER.

Late in the evening of March 2d, 1876, a carriage was driven up Wisconsin street and turned onto Jefferson street. About three minutes later I heard a report of a revolver and a minute later the carriage came down Wisconsin street, the horses on a run. Mrs. A. J. Wilner had called Dr. J. E. Garner to the door and shot him dead. She is still living and in an insane asylum. She was insane at the time of the tragedy. It was a case surrounded in a mystery which has not yet been satisfactorily solved as having been based upon any grounds other than the woman's insanity, and probably never will be.

CHARLEY KNOWLES' FIRE CRACKERS.

During the Blaine and Logan campaign the Republicans got pretty enthusiastic, had numerous meetings and parades and frequently made things howl well into the night. One night when they were out and indications were fair for a time or two, George Tillema came to me and said:

" 'Doc,' there is quite a lot of big fire crackers in my store. If any of the boys happen to want them to-night you sell them for twenty cents apiece."

About one o'clock in the morning I met Charley Knowles and three or four other enthusiasts who asked if I knew where they could get some fire crackers. I said I did, but they were the big cannon breed and would cost twenty cents each. Price cut no figure with them, so I unlocked the store and they took three dollars' worth, insisting that I take a pair of the weapons for my trouble. They went up near the corner of Jefferson and Wisconsin streets, I having assured them it was the proper time for the policeman on the beat to be at the farther end of his territory. As they went up the street I happened to think that Officer Mooney lived only a few doors away and, as I passed his house a short time before he was sitting by the fire reading a paper. I had a suspicion that if they did any shooting in his neighborhood he might fall out of the house and look after them, so I stopped at Milwaukee street and waited for developments.

"Bung," "Bang," "Bang," went three of the slumber disturbers and in about half a minute out came Mooney on a run. The boys walked leisurely across the street and met him. I touched a match to the centre of a fuse in a cracker, and about the time Mooney was preparing to run the boys in the thing went off.

"There," said Charley Knowles, "there's where your shooting is."

I had skipped up Milwaukee street a few doors and as I heard Mooney coming on the board walk, I ran down and met him at the corner.

"There they went, right down into the Third Ward," said I, and Mooney went in the direction I indicated on

a double quick. Then the boys lighted half a dozen
at once, shot themselves up Jefferson street and were a
block away before the things went off, and Mooney
came running back. He never suspected that I had
saved the real offenders from going to the station, but
the boys realized it. I had good cigars during a whole
week and George Tillema gave me fifty cents commission
on the sale of fire crackers.

OLD TIME POLICE.

One winter night an incident occurred which illus-
trated the efficiency of the old time police. The patrolmen went their beats by twos, same as detectives usually
do now. At least there were two to each of the down
town wards and there was no roundsman to keep tab on
them. They had their own way and went together if
they chose to.

There was a shop in the Seventh ward just over the
line from the Third in which a hard coal fire burned
nights. The patrolmen knew how to open the door and
usually those in the Third went up there in the small
hours to warm up. Occasionally those in the Seventh
ward also dropped in and the four would discuss topics
of the day or night.

One night when they were all in warming up there
was a fire in a dwelling house in the Third ward and it
burned to the ground without their knowledge. Later
the absence of policemen at the fire was reported at the
station and the Sergeant went out to hunt them. He
hunted me up and asked if I had seen them. I knew it
was all day with the boys if they were caught in the
shop, so I told him I thought they had chased some suspected thieve up through the Seventh ward some time
before but had just returned to their territory.

He went down in the Third ward to look after them
and I soon woke the boys up and told them the situation.
All four next morning reported an excited chase after
a brace of thieves away out into the vicinity of the dam,
where all traces of them were lost. There had been a
hot fire in the shop stove and they were all in a high

sweat. It hadn't cooled yet when they met the sergeant as they were trotting back to their beats. Whether it was the sweating or the lying that saved them hasn't been decided.

ROMANCE OF MASK BALLS.

In the years now behind us, mask balls were popular and the one of the season was always given at the Academy of Music, then owned by the Milwaukee Musical Society. Frequently there would be three or four popular ones in the city during a winter, and there were occasionally some ludicrous results.

One winter there was a leading business man living in the Seventh ward who was having some trouble at home. He and his wife were at outs and each was threatening to begin divorce proceedings.

The man was a fine looker, and the wife was never asked to play second fiddle to him in that respect. I was pretty familiar with the case and was thoroughly convinced it was one of unjustifiable jealousy, at least on the part of the husband. I often told him so but he refused to believe me.

One time, a couple of days prior to a mask ball, the wife went to Chicago to spend a week with her parents, the husband having refused to go to the ball, either with her or alone.

His wife, however, was little more than out of the city when he secured a ticket for himself and engaged an outfit of flashing apparel.

On the night of the ball, a few minutes before the grand march started, a carriage drove up hurriedly and a woman in a rich and dazzling garb of Persian royalty stepped out and hastened into the hall.

My discontented friend had not yet espied a partner to his exact fancy and was eagerly eyeing all late comers. As this particular one entered he was enraptured at once, hastened to her side and begged her company for the march. She as promptly accepted. Her every move was one of grace, elegance and refinement. He begged for her name, but she declined to give it, although, as

evidence of good faith he gave his. His only hope was
in being able to discover her identity after masks were
removed. But ere that hour arrived she had disappeared and the carriage had rolled away as rapidly as
it came. Who she was, whence she came or whither she
went was a mystery which refused to be solved.

When his wife returned from her visit, she was much

"The Real Object of Your Flattering Admiration."

pleased to learn from his own lips that he had not been
near the ball, and she seemed inclined to want to drop
all of their differences and make up.

But there was something upon the husband's mind.
A strange spirit seemed to haunt him.

A few days before the next mask ball Mrs. —— received a letter from her parents in Chicago urging herself and husband to be with them at a family gathering
on the evening the ball was to occur. Unfortunately he

had some important business engagements with business men from New York who were to be in Milwaukee that identical night and could not possibly accompany her to Chicago, much as he would like to, but insisted that she should not be deprived of the pleasure, and that she might as well go down the day previous.

On the night of the ball, at about the same moment in the hour as before, the same Persian royalty robed feminine form alighted from a carriage and entered the Academy of Music. Mr. —— was eyeing the door, animated by a high and throbbing hope and lost no time in getting to her side. Of course he was accepted. Again he worried his brain and her ear in a fruitless effort to learn who she was, but all he could get was permission to write her to a certain address, at the Milwaukee postoffice, general delivery.

Toward the time for unmasking he watched her closely, determined that she should not again escape him.

But she did, and the same carriage wheeled her away as rapidly and as mysteriously as before.

A couple of days later his wife returned and was again glad to learn that he had not attended the ball. His assurances of that fact seemed to animate her and she put forth special efforts to make home cheerful for him.

But somehow he wasn't happy. He appeared absent-minded, like, at times, and had to go to his office on business nearly every night. At the end of a month he had written at least a score of letters to Her Persian Royal Highness, and had detailed, several times over, his unhappy condition and the disconsolate state of his home and heart. He had received as many letters in return and they had grown full of sympathy for him in his enforced misery.

He had assured her that a divorce from all of his unhappiness was but a few months distant, at most, and had received permission to call upon her at a house in a fashionable neighborhood, on the west side at 8 o'clock on a certain evening.

He was there on time to a second and was ushered in by apparently the same form and clad in the same outfit of Persian royalty, even to the face mask. As he entered the house she said:

"You see I am interested, else I would not have taken the butler's place to usher you in."

He was delighted with that part of his welcome, but was grieved at not being permitted to look upon her face. Finally, after many entreaties and solemn promises on his part, she pulled off her face mask and he stood face to face with his colored housemaid.

For a moment he was as one stricken dumb and helpless. He attempted to arise from the chair, but was unable to do so. Before he was able to speak she said:

"My mistress felt herself unable to carry out this feature of her part of this grand and interesting farce comedy and I consented to usher you into her presence. Permit me to introduce you to the real object of your most flattering admiration. (the wife, entering the room) Mrs. ——."

That was the real squelcher and crusher of his spirits, he sank back in the chair and seemed upon the point of falling from it as his wife stood before him, her face beaming with a triumphant yet pitying smile as she looked him straight in the eye and said:

"George, from the very depths of my heart I pity you. I have been pitying you for a long time in our own home, and have been sympathizing with you as deeply and sincerely as I could through the postoffice, and my highest hope now is that out of all of this may come happiness and real home life to both of us. Here are all of your letters, and I trust you have all of mine. Every one of them was written in our own home and to that let us return with them and let their contents remain sacred between us."

"Sarah, tell James to drive up the carriage."

"Come George, let us go home. The comedy is ended. Let the curtain drop."

They went home and the foolishness ceased. Thereafter there was no happier couple in Milwaukee or one more devoted to each other. I have suppressed the names because they are both yet living, and in Wisconsin, though not in Milwaukee.

She had been in Chicago each time exactly as arranged, but, being advised of his movements, had come up to the ball on a train arriving at 8 o'clock and returned on one at 11 o'clock. The final act in the drama was performed in the home of another prominent business man, whose wife had been her classmate in college and who cheerfully gave her the full use of her drawing room and parlors for an hour, together with a solemn promise to ask no questions as to the purpose or outcome of the event. He confessed the whole story to me years after.

BURGLARIES.

During my twenty-five years experience as special policeman there have been three burglaries on my beat. Two of them occurred one Sunday afternoon when I was not on duty, and the other came one night about thirty days later. None of the burglars were caught and identified, but the man whose store was robbed in the night, and whose place was one of my charges, doubled my salary the next month. Somehow I never regarded that act in any other light than as appreciation of my ability to mind my own business.

SERGT. HOWARD'S FLY DIET.

Years ago, when Sergeant Howard, many years a member of the police force, occupied the position of roundsman, the Windsor Hotel was not kept in as good style as it now is, but it was a place where night men on the force were always welcome. It was long a custom of the house, as it should be of all well regulated hotels, to set out a warm lunch for them about midnight and the men would drop in and eat together. One hot night Roundsman Howard came in to lunch with the others. The light in the room was not very bright and after getting about half through with a bowl of soup he discovered that it was full of flies. He immediately went out and "Europed." That was the last of his soup eating there and he never suspected that any one in the party had swept up a handful of flies from a wall where they were roosting and salted his soup with them. In return for the night favors it was customary to send persons coming from late trians and inquiring for a hotel to the Windsor. Mr. Howard's diet of flies has always been a fresh spot in his memory.

JOHN M., AND HIS CANNON.

John M. Ewing once had a cannon at his command, a regular old bruiser which did service in the war of the Rebellion. It was at the close of the Blaine and Logan

" 'Doc,' The Devil is to Pay Here."

campaign when the result hung in the ballance for days, and Cleveland and Hendricks were finally declared elected.

Mr. Ewing had served as Secretary of the Republican State Central Committee and was confident of a Republican victory in the whole country. A few days before the election he sent to Madison and had one of the brass cannon which adorn the Capital park sent in for the purpose of firing a salute over the result.

On election night a big crowd of Republican saviors of the party and country were at the old Miner residence, then standing on the site of the Hotel Pfister, which was headquarters of a Republican club. Returns were being received there by a special wire. John had the cannon brought into the yard and left it there alone to be used at the proper time. He neither placed a guard over it nor took the ramrod away. During the evening I discovered it and carried the ramrod over to the Stafford store and put it inside.

Along about midnight I came around again. John and half a dozen other enthusiasts were out in the yard in a high state of excitement, searching for that ramrod. I had been around to Democratic headquarters and had seen a private dispatch to Ed. Wall, from New York, which satisfied me that it wouldn't be wise for John to do any shooting with that cannon that night. As I came into the yard John ran up to me and said:

" 'Doc,' the devil's to pay here! Somebody has stolen the ramrod to our gun. Blaine is elected and we can't start the celebration."

"So-o-o?" said I. "John, did you leave that gun out here without a guard? It's a wonder the enemy hasn't spiked it as well as stolen the ramrod."

John was in a great sweat. I called him aside and told him not to worry about the ramrod, or be in a hurry about celebrating unless he wanted to do something he wouldn't be proud of in his old age. He upbraided me a little for trifling with him, but nearly fainted when I told him the contents of the private dispatch I had seen. He concluded that it would be just as well to defer the shooting a little while and decided to tell the crowd inside it was because the ramrod had been stolen, but that he had sent a man to make a new one which would be there in less than an hour.

Before the hour was up the Republicans received information which fully reconciled them to the idea of deferring the shooting, and John M. Ewing still insists that I saved him from disgracing himself by celebrating a Democratic victory, through my cussèdness in stealing the ramrod to his cannon.

SUTTER'S ELECTRIC LIGHTS.

The first electric light that glimmered in Milwaukee

was owned by a photographer named Harry Sutter. He
had a gallery on the top floor across Milwaukee street
from the postoffice and he was a genuine genius. He
got his apparatus in shape and produced a brilliant light.
Then he got a strong reflector by which he could throw
the light any reasonable distance and land it where he
pleased. One night he trained it on a window of Henry
Wehr's saloon at No. 1, Grand avenue and, though the
distance was four ordinary blocks, he poked a glow of
light through that window which made the crowd present
hop around as though a ball of lurid lightning had
dropped among them.

Harry was watching for the effect, and before the dis-
turbed ones had time to locate the cause of disturbance,
he slipped a black card board before the light and waited
for matters to become quiet. After a few minutes he let
the light on again, just long enough to raise a commo-
tion. He kept up that sort of play for nearly an hour,
until the placid temper of Henry Wehr actually became
ruffled and, after much perseverance he was able to locate the light, then he put on his coat and hat and started
out to squelch the long range intruder.

As Henry was passing the lamp post at Broadway and
Wisconsin street, Harry discovered him and suspected
some disturbance at his end of the show, if he wasn't
headed off. In half a minute he shifted the reflector and
dropped the light plump into Henry's face just as he
was at the hallway at 107 Wisconsin street. Henry was
nearly blinded by the dazzling glimmer and dodged into
the hallway to escape it.

Harry saw the movement and turned the light, with
full force, upon the stairway entrance. Then he slipped
out, locked the door, ran down two flights of stairs, then
down Milwaukee to Michigan street and around and up
Broadway to Wisconsin. He then walked up Wisconsin
street to where the popular saloon keeper was a prisoner
and asked him what was the matter. Henry was trembling and said he believed an electric gattling gun was
trained upon him from that d—d photographer's place.

Harry said he suspected it was a young fellow who
was learning photography up there and who was playing

with a big lamp and looking glass reflector, but as he knew Mr. Sutter very well he would go up and ask him to stop the annoyance.

"Py dunder," said Henry, "eef I know him purty well, I lick him like blitzen the first time I catch him on the street. He haf spoilt my peesiness for the night already vonce."

Henry refused to leave his fortification until the light was turned off and Harry often said he believed his adroitness saved him from a thumping.

NEWSPAPER ROOST.

Away back in the old time newspaper days of the Republican and News the newspaper men of the city had a sort of club room in which there were some pieces of green top furniture and other things not constructed exactly like writing desks. The then manager of the roost now ranks pretty well up, in the papers, as a Michigan editor. Whatever was done in that place was done and no disturbing hand was raised against it. The newspaper men were, of course, on good terms with the brewers and pretty nearly every brewery distributing wagon which passed that way left a case of beer at the foot of the stairs. There were some people who thought that was not a good place to leave beer, especially in hot weather, as it might get too warm, or in cold weather, as it might freeze. However that might have been, the night policeman and watchmen and some other people in that locality were seldom short of a bottle of beer when they wanted it. They rather appreciated the manager's neglect to take care of the beer when it was delivered.

SHE DIDN'T DO WASHING.

Away back in the days when Policeman Dodge was station keeper in the old police station I had a bit of experience with a buxom young woman in it. It was about 2:30 o'clock on a summer morning and the first streaks of approaching day were beginning to show in the east. She came down Wisconsin street with a big market basket full of clothes on her arm and a pair of shoes tied to the handle of the basket.

"Good morning, my good woman," said I, "you are out early for your day's washing."

"Well, I may be out early, but I don't do washing," she retorted with a snap in her tone.

"Will, I Don't Do Washing."

That was her fatal mistake. If she'd said: "Yis sor, and Oi'm hurryin' away to Miss Grane's on Twinty-third strate, so to git the job done and be home in time to git dinner," she would have been all right.

"O, you don't do washing? Beg jour pardon, madam, but I thought from appearance that perhaps you did washing," said I.

"Well, I don't do washing," she snapped.

"But, if you don't do washing, what do you do with so large a basket of clothes as that at this time of night?" I asked walking along at her side.

"Well, I don't do washing, and that settles it," was her reply.

I walked along with her and kept her talking until we walked into the old police station, where she told Dodge a highly plausible story about having a sister living somewhere on Fourth street for whom she was looking. Dodge gave her a cot in the women's department and in the morning she went out to look for her sister. In about an hour a message came from the Industrial school that a girl had escaped during the night and stolen a lot of clothes. Officer Pat Howe was detailed to look after her and, about noon, found her in Wauwatosa, waiting to take a train for her home in Portage.

ONE ON MR. HANNIFIN.

Not all of the good things I have discovered materialized in the night. I usually go down town in the afternoon and, from force of habit. I presume, linger around the Chapman store, in former years, frequently going inside and taking a general look through the store, so I would know the location of things if anything occurred in the night.

One day when I was in the store Manager Hannifin was in a high rage. It seemed he had ordered a lot of printed matter, which was to have been delivered nearly a week before and it hadn't come yet. He had sent a messenger to the printing office, who brought back the announcement that the job would be done next day. That set Mr. Hannifin on edge and he made use of several new combinations of very impressive cuss words over the delay.

A few minutes after the printer who had the job in hand came in with a proof sheet of the work and went to the head of the department in which it was to be used to have it approved. As he started to leave, the head of the department remarked:

"Mr. Hannifin is hotter than a furnace about this job not having been done on time and swears it is the last job you will ever get from this store. Don't let him see you. Keep out of sight until he cools off. There he is now! Get in the office here and hide behind a desk until he goes off the floor!"

"It's a Terror of a Place. Uh, uh, O!"

"Not much," said John. "You just watch my smoke."

John had entered the store at a lively gait, indicating perfect health in body and limb. Instantly he clapped a hand on his right hip and began hobbling toward the manager apparently in great agony and hardly able to navigate.

"Hello, John, what the devil is the matter with you?" asked the manager.

"Say, Mr. Hannifin, I think you ought to have a lot

of salt or ashes scattered on that walk out there," said John. "It is awful bad. If some woman had fallen on it she might have been terribly injured and you'd have a big damage suit on your hands. O! O! Ouch!" and he fairly writhed with agony and rubbed his hip and back.

"What? Did you fall?" asked Mr. Hannifin.

"Fall? I should say I did. It's a terror of a place; uh, uh, O!" said John.

"Really, I hope you are not badly hurt," said the manager, his heart melting in sympathy.

"Hurt! Uh, uh, O! You can feel a big lump there on my back now. Don't know as I'll be able to get home," said John. "What I came over for, Mr. Hannifin, was to see you about that job of printing. We've been delayed a little getting the paper and I was afraid you would be angry and quit us."

"O, no, no. That's all right. You know we'd not forsake you, John. No hurry about it. Any time this week will do. Really, I hope you are not seriously hurt. Let me call a carriage to take you home or to a doctor," urged Mr. Hannifin, becoming thoroughly alarmed.

"No, no, no," said John. "I'll manage to get back to the office. But I was afraid you'd be angry about the job."

"Never fear about that. Just count yourself in on a perpetual contract for all of our work as long as I am here. Let me know how you are getting along to-morrow," said Mr. Hannifin.

And John hobbled out of the store and kept up the limping until he got around the corner out of sight. The clerks who had witnessed the interview and caught on to the situation were ready to burst with laughter, but held their peace, and I doubt if to this day Mr. Hannifin knows that one of the smoothest pantomimes and confidence schemes of the age was played upon him right in the big store of which he is the manager.

ATTEMPTED ROBBERY AT 416.

Here is one which is a trifle too new to require the use of names. The circumstances are still quite fresh in the minds of quite a number of persons.

A woman had rooms on Milwaukee street not a bolck from the headquarters of the Associated Charities. She also had a fine array of diamonds and was reported as carrying considerable money with her constantly. One night as she was going to her rooms a man seized her in the second floor hall, threw her to the floor and proceeded to try to rob her of her diamonds and money. She screamed wildly and, being unable to smother her noise, the would be robber became alarmed, and rushed down the stairs, the woman close at his heels shouting:

"Thief! Murder; Robber! Stop you villain!"

Quite a number of persons who had heard her cries were running toward the place. As the robber broke across the street they followed him and he was captured at the police patrol barn on Oneida street and locked up in the station. He had failed to get either the woman's diamonds or money.

The fellow was held in jail for trial, but I don't remember of having ever seen in print any report of his trial.

JOE HORWITZ AND THE BURGLAR.

Did you ever stop by a large plate glass window, in the night, put the tip of a finger along the glass, press pretty snug and drive your finger along the glass at a sort of stuttering or jumping-sliding gait? Just try it some night when there is a clerk alone in the rear part of the store and then get him to try to describe to you the fiendish noise it makes.

I tried it one night, years ago, when one Phillips had a shoe store where the Hanan De Muth shoe store now is. "Joe" Horwitz was clerking for Phillips and was in the rear of the store alone shining his shoes preparatory to going out to an 11 o'clock engagement. As my finger went across the glass "Joe" wouldn't have dropped that shoe brush quicker if it had been a red hot brick and came out of the store on a run. I fell back a few steps and was just advancing again leisurely as he came out, pale, trembling and so frightened he could scarcely speak. Running up to me he said, panting for breath:

"Uh, Uhu, hu, 'D—Doc!' There's a burglar in the store."

"O, pshaw," said I, "it's another case of cats. There's no burglar in there."

"Ye-yes there is," said he, "right back there in the office. 'Si—'si was blacking my shoes he yelled at me in the most hellish voice 'J-J-Joe-o-o-o!' He's in there, sure. I wouldn't go back there for a thousand dollars."

"Well, go on away, then," said I, "and have your time. "I'll take care of the store and the burglar, too."

And he went, at a lively gait, looking back about every ten steps until he was a block away, confidently expecting a burglar to come out and shoot me. I locked the door, which he had forgotten to do, and, out of mercy to "Joe," kept the story to myself.

SOME GOOD ONES ON ME.

Not all of the jokes and tricks played upon persons on my beat have been at the expense of others. I have been the victim my share of the time. Jake Janssen, of Ladd & Janssen, and Herman Hammersmith, in Camp's jewelry store, got one on me once. Ladd & Janssen received a consignment of choice wine. I paid for a couple of bottles and ordered them sent to my house, for a special occasion close at hand. The occasion came and I pulled the corks. The bottles contained only Lake Michigan water which costs about seven cents a thousand gallons. Hammersmith had suggested emptying out the wine and filling the bottles with water. After a while they asked how my wine was and I replied:

"O, I lost the whole of it. Hired girl put it in the refrigerator to get cold and a cake of ice fell on the bottles and crushed both of them. At least she said so, and I guess it was so, for I saw her clearing the broken bottles out from the ice."

Not so long ago but I remember it very distinctly Mr. Hammersmith wanted to sell me a bicycle. I took rather kindly to the idea and he said if I would go up to the Farwell avenue riding school and learn to ride he would deduct the cost at the school from the price of the wheel. I thought it would be rather nice to ride a wheel home and surprise my family, so I went up to the school and learned. I did it all in one afternoon, but my hands were blistered and torn, my knees were skinned and I was pretty nearly pounded into a mass of pulp. I took care of my beat that night, went to bed in the morning and remained there for three days with one of the worst cases of rheumatism I ever had. I also had a plenty of riding a wheel. All of the roseate hue on the idea of surprising my family on a wheel had vanished, like flowers that bloom in the spring.

A few years ago a stranger shot himself in a hallway on Milwaukee street. It was early in the evening and his body was soon found. I promptly identified him as Col. Charley Wheeler. A messenger was sent to Mr. Wheeler's house to notify his family and, to the messenger's surprise, Mr. Wheeler opened the door. The real identity of the suicide has not yet been learned.

SPONTANEOUS COMBUSTION.

I once discovered an actual case of spontaneous combustion. There was opportunity for two cases, but only one materialized. A woman pretty well known in Milwaukee had manicure rooms on Wisconsin street. In connection with them were her private parlor and sleeping room. One morning about 2 o'clock, as I was on the opposite side of the street, she came hurriedly down stairs and excitedly called to me to come over there, quick. I ran across the street and she said there must be a fire in the building as her rooms were full of smoke.

I ran up the stairs and opened the door. There was no blaze in sight, but the room was quite thick with smoke. I at once suspected it was a smoulderer, only waiting for a draft of air to start a blaze. Scratching a match I began to investigate. On a rear window sill was a bunch of waste from which smoke was issuing and there was a strong odor of linseed oil. I picked up a water pitcher and drenched the waste. There was a hissing sound, as though the water had struck hot metal.

Being satisfied that was the source of the smoke, I

opened the windows and the smoke soon disappeared. Investigation showed that the woman had oiled a portion of the floor after 9 o'clock that night, rubbing the oil on with a handful of cotton waste, and then had laid the waste on the window sill, on top of half a dozen iron screw eyes, a piece of brass or copper wire and a handful of rusty nails. In five hours spontaneous combustion had developed.

The woman had been asleep and her lungs were pretty well filled with smoke. Sitting at an open window gave her some relief, but she thought a swallow of brandy was necessary. I trotted off to a drug store and got her a four ounce bottle full. She got outside of the brandy and was soon all right. As I was leaving she wanted to know who I was, declared I had saved her life and wanted to reward me, then and there, but being paid by property owners for my services I was forced to decline the reward offered.

A CASE OF DEAF AND DUMB.

Some years ago a deaf and dumb man worked both sides of the street for several months. He had a pitiful story on his slate and the kind hearted contributed liberally. I had watched him some time and came to the conclusion he could talk if he wanted to. One afternoon I caught him in another part of town. His coat was buttoned over his slate. He went into a saloon. So did I, but paid no attention to him, and ordered a beer. Suddenly I turned and invited him to have one. He heard instantly, responded promptly and talked freely. I reported the fact to the station and he was taken in a day or two later. He had in his grip at his boarding house between $600 and $700 in gold. That ended his impositions upon Milwaukee people.

A COSTLY CANDIDACY.

"Ed." Hackett, "Tom" Ramsey and a few others of the old set in which they travelled in former years, once put up a very successful job on Fred Callis. It was when Fred kept a saloon on Milwaukee street, between Wisconsin and Michigan streets and had a good stock of the best imported goods. A city election was approaching and there was considerable talk about Aldermanic candidates. In those days only a saloon man stood any show of an election in the Third ward.

One night the crowd in question went to Fred's place at about 11 o'clock, seated themselves in a private room and entered into an apparent earnest consultation. Instead of the usual Milwaukee brew, they ordered a bottle of Champagne. Callis nearly fell over at the order, but the boys were good payers and being the only ones then in the house, he gave his best attention.

When Fred came in with the order, room for another had been provided at the table and he was invited to the vacant seat. Proper gravity was observed and as the second filling of the glasses was ready for use one of the party informed Mr. Callis that they were there on no less important business than that of a committee from Democratic headquarters with instructions to secure his consent to become a candidate for alderman for the Third ward, assuring him of the most hearty support and a certainty of the nomination, if he would accept it.

The proposition had the proper swelling effect upon the head of the innocent Michlenberger, which was considerably enhanced by the further announcement that the decision had been made that the Irish in the ward, who had always ruled it in the council, would give him their united support, following the lead of Hacket, Ramsey and the other lights of the party. After due consideration Fred gave his consent to accept the nomination. During the discussion a full dozen bottles of Champagne were put out of sight, all furnished by the house, in recognition of the honor about to be conferred upon its head.

The matter was left for a further consultation the next night, when other party leaders were to be present, and Fred was cautioned to keep profoundly silent about it until all details could be arranged.

The next night the crowd was so much increased by leading lights in the party that it took two bottles to go around. The conference was quite lengthy and about two dozen bottles were emptied, all in recognition of the coming honor. The proceeding was kept up about ten days before all details were arranged. During the time the party lights consumed over 200 bottles of Fred's Champagne, and large numbers of best cigars, all at his expense. During the last few days prior to the nominating convention Fred's candidacy became known and he received the congratulations of nearly everybody in the Third ward, as well as of large delegations from other parts of the city, all of whom, of course, were properly entertained. His candidacy cost Callis something over $700 and when the time came, of course an Irishman was nominated. Germany was as far from receiving recognition as it had ever been before or as it has been since in the Third ward.

THE CHAPMAN STORE FIRE.

I recall the night of the fire in the Chapman store. About a quarter of ten as I was passing the front I thought there was a suspicious look around the gas jet burning at the rear of the store. Every watchman knows more fires have been discovered through smoke around a burning gas jet than in any other way. I watched it and my suspicion grew stronger that something was wrong. The fire chief had often told me to take no chances, so I ran to the nearest fire box and pulled in an alarm.

The fire laddies came flying, and by the time they arrived there was plenty of fire. Before morning $600,-000 worth of property had gone up in smoke.

Next morning Mr. Chapman stood on the opposite corner. Some of his lady clerks were there lamenting over the great loss. Turning to them, he said:

"See here, ladies; the store is gone, but I am here yet. Worse things than that might happen."

A Miss Davis said to me: "Mr. Aubery, unless I mistake the man there will be a new store built here inside of six months."

She was right. On the 6th of the following April

occurred the opening of the new store, which still occupies its position as one of the finest institutions of the kind in the West, and a grand monument to the skill and energy of the man whose efforts made it.

LEG OF THE TABLE.

One winter a company of Seventh ward young bloods set out to organize a minstrel show. They had a couple

"Let's Get Him Out of Here and Thaw Him Out."

of rooms in which to rehearse, the same rooms as have for some years been occupied by W. C. Williams as a law office, just across the alley from Heyn's store. Among their paraphernalia was a dummy man, stuffed with shavings. After a few rehearsals they bursted up, quit the business and threw the dummy out through the window into the alley. Not long after, I came that way and discovered the dummy in the alley. Having been in the rooms one night during rehearsal, I readily understood what it was. There was a snow squall on at the time and I straightened Mr. Dummy along the side of the building and went away.

Policeman McCormick was then on the Third ward beat and I watched for him. In about an hour he came along and I said to him:

"Mc., there's some poor devil laid out down here in the alley. I guess we'd better go and take care of him."

McCormick was agreed and we went to the alley to save the fellow from freezing. As Mc. looked at the prostrate form he said:

"Ah, sure, an' Oi know who it is right well. Sure, it's 'Lig of The Table'."

"Leg of The Table" was a nick-name by which a certain Third ward character was known.

"Well, 'Mc.'," said I, "let's get him out of here and take him to the station and thaw him out. You get hold of his shoulders and I'll take his legs and we'll carry him out."

As "Mc." got his grip on the shoulders the thing fell apart and the shavings scattered out in the alley. McCormick's disgust and chagrin at being sold and having identified the thing was inexpressible. He stood and looked at the wreck fully a minute and then said:

" 'Doc' Ahbry, yez can laugh much as ye loik, but Oi say thot was a dhirty blaggairdin' thrick. Oi w'uldn't moind the joke, but fur hevin, ixprissed me poshitive belaif thot it was 'Lig of The Table,' so Oi w'uldn't."

POOR LITTLE ORPHANS.

A good many years ago there was an organization in the city known as the Poor Little Orphans club. It was composed of a lot of wealthy men, such as James Petley, Q. A. Matthews, I. G. Mann, E. O. Riddell, Rufus Allen, and others of that class, all of Yankee birth. During winter months they usually held a meeting and had a dance each Friday night, always in Severances' hall. Their meetings were of the real, old, down east Yankee sociable order and their lunch always consisted of doughnuts, pumpkin pie and cider. One evening's supply was usually a bushel of doughnuts, a dozen pies and two to four gallons of cider, which they always got by the barrel from York state. They were a jolly set and never required the presence of a policeman to keep order. The club was one of the pleasant organizations which came and has gone during my time as guardian of mercantile interests in the nights of twenty-five years.

A MASHER MASHED.

Not very long ago a Seventh ward dude took a stroll down Wisconsin street on a mashing expedition. He is an inveterate smoker, and smokes only the best Barrister cigars. He stepped up to a healthy looking young woman who was passing up the street and in an instant I saw an umbrella descending upon his head with a muscular feminine arm at the helm. She not only pounded him over the head, but jabbed him in the ribs and soon gave him the worst of the deal. I said to myself: "That's the kind of girl who ought to come around here oftener." I finally went to his rescue, about the time the girl went triumphantly away, assured him he had been treated badly and advised him to go to a Barber shop, as the police were onto his game and might run him in.

POLICEMAN LOST AN EAR.

Back in the old days there were some high times in the Third ward. It was justly entitled to be called "The Bloody Third." It held some of the toughest nuts the town ever harbored. After there had been several times and pieces of times down there in swift succession a burly policeman was sent into the territory to straighten things out. The "laddiebucks" were a trifle suspicious of him and kept in line for awhile. But finally "de b'ys" got out for a time and he dropped upon them right in the midst of trouble.

Immediately there was a change of front on the part of the combatants. The contending forces ceased their

contentions and lined up as one man against the "cop."
He came out of the melee minus an ear and wearing
various other wounds and blemishes. One of the old
Third's thoroughbreds had bitten off the ear.

A few days after one old resident of the ward remarked to another:

"Gud mornan', Mr. O'Brine. Oi hear yer bye has
got in trouble wid a polaceman."

"Indade he have, sir," said Mr. O'B., and Oi do be
thinkin' it's a purty bad mess he's in, so Oi do."

"And do he still be havin' the aer phat he bit off the
affisher?"

"Yis, he have that same; he have it tacked on the
corner av the house as a warnin' til the nixt cop phat
do be sint into the warrud."

"Yis, Mr. O'Brine; but if the polaceman do be dyin',
you'll have to shoot the bye. Sure Oi did be hearin'
that same this mornin', down to Paddy the Jews."

"Bedads, if the polaceman doies, then let him come
afther the bye an' take 'is own revange," said Mr.
O'Brien.

FELLOWS MADE HAPPY.

Not all of my discoveries have turned out bad or been
without pleasant memories connected.

One night, a lot of years ago, Mr. A. B. Severance,
the owner of Severance hall, came to me and said:

" 'Doc,' I wish you'd keep an eye on my hall nights."

"Why, what's matter?" said I.

"Well," said he, "I think there's somebody sleeping
up there on the third floor, nights, just outside the danc-
ing hall door."

"Owl right," said I; "I'll look after 'em."

About 2 o'clock next morning I went up the stairs
to the third floor and I had him. There lay a lad about
a dozen years old, sound asleep. I yanked him up and
said:

"What'n thundernation ye doin' here? This is no
place for you to sleep. Come out of here and go to the
station."

The little fellow began to beg not to be taken to the station and then began to cry. That was too much for me. When the little fellow began to squak I weakened and thought he was some mother's boy and was not personally responsible for his being, or for being homeless. So I took him to a warm place where he could sleep till morning and then took him home with me. In a day or two I got him a job in the Sentinel office at three dollars a week. My wife fixed up his clothes, made him some more and we gave him a home until things shaped differently for him. He cut up a few capers that were not quite on the square, but finally got down to business, got some education and is now a Milwaukee business man and doing well.

Another youngster in whom I took an interest, hasn't forgotten it. He was a little fellow, one of two small brothers. Their mother was a widow and sickly and the two little ones were working to support her. The one I picked up was carrying messages for the Western Union telegraph office. I got acquainted with him, learned his history, saw he was made of the right stuff and one night asked him if he wouldn't like a better job. He said that was just what he did want so he could earn more for his dear mother. Next day I got him a job in a grocery store where he got much better wages. He grew up working in that store, and is now a traveling salesman for one of the largest whol sale grocery houses in the state, lives in a northern Wisconsin city and has a fine family.

One day not long ago a fine looking man came to me on the street and said:

"How are you, 'Doc?' I am very glad to see you, for I owe you a lot."

"Guess you're a little off," said I. "I don't recollect ever lending you a quarter."

"Neither do I," said he, "but I do remember when I was a friendless little kid carrying messages for $1.50 a week and trying to live, and you got me a job as bell boy at the Kirby house at $3 a week and board. That was my start and set me up in life. I'm running a big insurance office in Chicago now; got a fine home and a nice family, and I owe it all to you. Wish you'd come to Chicago, stay a month and be my guest. You bet I'll never forget you and my job at the old Kirby. Come and see me; give me a chance and I will try to reciprocate."

But my pick ups haven't all been boys. O, you think something now, do you? Well you're off again. I've left the other fellows to do the picking up of the she boys.

One day while looking around town I dropped into a hotel on the east side. An intelligent looking man was sitting alone. I casually dropped down by him and said, "howdy." He responded and I saw at once that he had a case of blues. It didn't take me long to find that he was a foreigner, just arrived here, was a physician and financially short. After a few minutes talk I said to him:

"Come 'long 'n' take little walk with me,'t'll do ye good."

Somehow he seemed to have a bit of confidence and came. I took him up street to a drug store, introduced him to two resident physicians and suggested that they give him a bit of a show. He is one of the prominent physician of the city now and has often told me that I caught him on the verge of the barren pastures of despair and turned him into a clover patch which had no fence around it.

But not all of my finds were of this agreeable finish kind. I'll make a chapter somewhere in this book of some of the others.

T. A. CHAPMAN.

At the time of the soldier's reunion here, in 1880, I made application to Mr. Chapman and other merchants, for a week's furlough. When I said to him: "Mr. Chapman, I want to get off duty for a week," he looked at me and replied: "What? Why, that's just the time you ought to be on duty."

"Now, see here," said I, "you take into consideration the fact that I put down the rebellion and taught more'n half of the Wisconsin troops the manual of arms, and was right there every time they won a victory, from start to finish, and you know very well if I were chained to that lamp post the boys would release me. You can bet on that."

"Say no more, say no more," said he; "it is all right. Put a good man on the beat and enjoy yourself."

So it was, and we had a good time.

T. A. Chapman was a part of the noblest work of God. He was loved by all who knew him. After many years of the hardest work and getting his business in proper shape he made Mr. Mills manager of the store, thus getting for himself some relief. Then he took to being out of doors much, for recreation and health. And he seemed to take an interest in everybody's welfare. He purchased some property on Jackson street and prepared to build upon it. He was there much of the time superintending the work and enjoyed it.

I had recently bought a little home which abutted against his property. One day I was out in the yard fixing up a chicken house when he saw me and came over and this is about the conversation which followed.

"What are you doing over there, 'Doc?'"

"Hello! Is that you, Mr. Chapman? O, just fixing up my chicken coop. Looks like I am going to have some new neighbors, see? and I don't want to lose any of my white Leghorns."

He took in the situation, for he always liked an innocent joke.

"Why don't you fill your lot up there a little, bring it to a level, move the barn over on the line and fix it up in shape?" said he.

"Now, look here," said I, "I've just got my little home paid for, but have no money in the bank. Another year, if I can, I intend to do just that same thing, b'gosh."

"O, that's it, is it?" said he.

"Yes, sir; that's the size of the pile and just what's troublin' Hannah and yours truly," said I.

He ran his fingers through his hair, as he was accustomed to do when thinking, looked me in the eye and said:

"Look here, 'Doc', you go up to Owen Goss, the house mover, and see what it will cost you to have that work done, and done right. D'ye hear? Let me know in two days."

The third day following I met him at the same place and he said:

"Well, 'Doc,' did ye find out about that business?"

"Yes, sir; I did," said I.

"How much will it cost?" he asked.

"Ninety-eight dollars and fifty cents, sir," said I.

"O, 'twill, will it? Look here, you go and have that done right off. Send me the bill and I will make you a present of it. Don't let them rob us down at the store."

That was Timothy A. Chapman, my employer, who was a poor boy himself once, but who proved himself one of the noblest works of God, an honest, good man.

It is not strange that there was general mourning when he died. His life history was full of just such acts as the one I have related.

WHERE I CAUGHT A THIEF.

Years ago, I lived on the west side, out on Third street. My usual route down to my beat was across Oneida street bridge. One cold night I met a fellow on the bridge with a buffalo robe under his arm. I wobbled around just a trifle and as I met him said:

"H'war ye? What got, eh? Buf'lo, eh? Want sell 't?"

He allowed he didn't want to sell it, as he had just brought it with him from Denver and was taking it home. I bantered him for a price on it and he finally said: "Ten dollars."

I wanted the robe mighty badly, but had only five dollars with me. But I had a friend only a block up the street who would lend me the other five. He finally consented to go back and get the money and in a couple of minutes we walked into the old police station. Lieut. Kendrick was on duty and stretched back in his chair as we walked in. Giving him a signal squint with my larboard eye I said:

"Cap'n, I want t' buy this man's buf'lo robe for ten

dollars and only got five with me. 'll ye lend me five till morn'n?"

He said he'd lend me the five and keep the robe for security. That was satisfactory and he got up, took the robe and walked the fellow into a cell. Next day he was sentenced for six months.

Less than ten minutes before E. R. Pantke had been in and reported the theft of a buffalo robe from a hook in front of his store and several officers had been sent out to look for the thief. The balance of that winter I wore a pair of warm fur gloves, a present from Pantke.

DAN DAGGETT ON FREE LUNCH.

About 3 o'clock one morning, Dan Daggett, in his normal condition for that hour, had full possession of the Wisconsin street sidewalk, on the postoffice side, and was water-logging up the street toward his rooms. He was the same Dan that, one other morning, kicked a defenseless skunk off the sidewalk, mistaking it for a cat.

Earlier in the night a bill poster had spilled a bucket of paste on the sidewalk, and it made a big, gray puddle. Dan approached the mess, rolling like an old schooner in a heavy sea, braced himself, cocked his head to the left and looked at it and blurted out:

" 'At fel' mus' struck mighty big free lunch, hic, b'gosh. Damfool, might known couldn't git 't all home 'ith 'im."

EXPERIENCE WITH A MAD DOG.

There was, in my early years on the street, a pretty thorough sport in town known as Harry. He was a genuine rounder and could carry more booze in his tank and not show it than any other three fellows in the city Harry had two dogs, one a pretty fair-sized bull, the other apparently a cross between a water spaniel and a Scotch terrier. They knew his haunts as well as he did and would take his trail at Tenth street and locate him in some one of the half-dozen saloons then on Milwaukee street at any hour, day or night. Harry was a thorough stayer and comer. He was last to turn in at night and first around in the morning.

A good-natured Irishman kept a saloon in the Third ward, just south of the Seventh ward line. He took considerable pains to make things pleasant for the boys, and for a time held a good share of their patronage.

Early in August another Irishman opened a saloon in a basement a couple of doors away. He was up to his business and understood the importance of a round on the house frequently. It wasn't long until the crowd drifted to his place as headquarters, practically deserting his countryman, who had a just claim to priorty of location on the street.

The mixer of jag seed who had been deserted by the crowd for a new love felt the abandonment keenly and offered two thoroughly alive Third ward chaps all the drinks they wanted for a month free, if they would play a good joke on the new comer and chase the gang out of his place.

It was right in the heat of dog days and there had been several mad dog stories in the papers. One sultry night, about 10 o'clock, Harry's dogs came down on his trail. The fellows for whom the free drinks were in store were lying for them. They inviegled them into a back room a few doors distant where they had a bucket of foamy lather made with a cake of soap just on the market, which was warranted to make a lather that would hold its foam an hour. This lather they slashed over the head, neck, mouth and shoulders of the larger dog and then let them out.

The dogs made a bee line for the new saloon, went in on the bound and flew around the room in search of their master. At that moment one of the conspirators stuck his head over the stairway by the open door and yelled:

"Mad dog! Mad dog! Look out there!"

As the eyes of the crowd caught on the dog with its head and neck flecked with foam there was a tumult of yells and a rush for the door. The shouting frightened the dogs and they also made for the door. The rear guard of the rush grabbed a chair and by one swoop

sent both dogs to the rear of the room and the crowd
escaped onto the street. Every one was fully convinced
it was a genuine mad dog. Half an hour later most of the
gang were in the saloon of their first love where the two
who worked the game regaled them with blood curdling
stories about the narrow escapes of half a dozen persons
from the jaws of that same dog as he came down through
the First and Seventh wards.

Next day the daily papers all had the story of the
mad dog and the narrow escape of a score of persons.
Before the fellows got onto the joke they had forsaken
the new saloon entirely and the other fellow had a flour-
ishing trade again.

AN ESCAPED LUNATIC.

It was about 2 o'clock one September morning, the
sky clear and the air just a trifle cool. As I crossed
from the Chapman store and started down Wisconsin
street I saw coming up the street an athletic built fellow
fully six feet high, and well proportioned. He acted a
little queer, I thought, as he seemed to be watching in
every direction. I walked towards him and as he came
near he darted into a hallway and ran part way up the
dark stairs. As I came up to the entrance he said:

"Don't shoot! For God's sake don't!" and there was
a piteous tone to his appeal.

My first thought was that he was some fellow with
a case of the fruits of over-indulgence in flim-flam
whisky, vulgarly known as "jim jams, or snakes," and
said:

"What's matter, old man? Who's goin' to shoot?
Nobody's going to shoot you while I am here; you can
bet on that."

"Is that so?" he asked, "are you my friend?"

"You bet I am," said I, "what made you think I was
going to shoot?"

"'Cause I met another fellow down the road and he
threatened to shoot me. I thought everybody was going to shoot."

"No; nobody wil shoot you. Come on down here and

let's talk the matter over," said I.

He came down the stairs and looked wildly in every direction and I saw at once that his head had gone wrong. It was about time for the regular officer to come along and my play was to interest him until reinforcements arrived. So I went at him in a matter of fact way, not appearing to watch him at all.

"What's your name?" I asked.

"Adam," was his reply.

"Adam? Adam what? Nothing but just Adam?" I asked.

"That's all," said he, "just Adam. You've heard about me, ain't you. I owned a farm out here a couple of miles. My first wife's name was Eveline. The neighbors called her 'Eve.' She got me into trouble with my landlord, a long time ago, and I got a divorce from her. I've got along better since."

"O, yes;" said I, "I remember about you now. Where you been living lately?"

"Don't live anywhere," said he, "just stay wherever I happen to be."

"By this time I concluded that it was a bad case on my hands and I had a growing desire for the appearance of the regular officer on the beat, yet I couldn't foretell what effect the sight of another person might have on him. He was getting uneasy and was liable to break away any minute. Seeing that some move must be made I asked:

"Where was it that fellow threatened to shoot you?"

"Right down this road, just this side of the woods, right there near the milldam, where the stump fence runs up against the stone wall," said he.

"Then we'd better take a walk this way," said I, "and come around the other side of the woods, or, if you like, I'll take you over to my house and give you a bed. I don't want anybody to shoot you."

He was agreed and we walked up Milwaukee street to Mason, then down to Broadway and in ten minutes poor Mr. Adam was in a cell in the police station. He was one of the most dangerous lunatics at the Wauwatosa asylum and had escaped that night. Next morning it took six good men to handle him and get him back to the asylum, where the poor fellow died the next year.

BOY BAILED OUT.

Fifteen to twenty years ago there was a young sport, son of a wealthy citizen, who was often getting himself into trouble. About once a month he would send for me to come over and bail him out of the police station. He always fixed matters up next day and I felt it a sort of duty to help him out. After a while his father learned what was going on. He hunted me up and said:

"Look here, 'Doc,' if you want to have any comfort around this town don't you bail that boy of mine out of the station again. Just you tell them to send for me next time."

Of course, I obeyed and said nothing, but, some way, the boy caught on and kept straight for quite a while, but one night up came a messenger boy with a request for a deposit of $31.

"O, no;" said I, "not this time. I have my orders. Go and tell his father."

Next day, just before the "consolation carriage" left for the House of Correction, Willie was bailed out and sent out west to grow up with the country. He is now a prosperous business man in St. Paul.

INCIDENTS WITH FIRES.

There have been a good many incidents in connection with fires. Some of them have been too serious to discuss lightly. One of that kind occurred at the fire in Charley Kraus' saloon, near the Academy of Music.

A fire occurred at the same place a few years before, when a dressmaker who had rooms on the second floor was overcome by smoke and firemen carried her down a ladder. As was the case with Mrs. Kraus, she had plenty of time to have gotten down the stairs, but got rattled and didn't know what to do.

In the olden times small fires were occasionally extinguished without calling out the department. The regular policeman and I discovered one in the rear part of a small store on Mason street. A kerosene lamp had gone wrong and the blaze around it was just starting. We kicked the door open and put out the fire with a pail of water which was in the store.

The owner of the building lived over the store. Our kicking the door open awoke him. He slipped into his trowsers, ran to the police station and said there were burglars in Munn's store. Two policemen came back with him on a run, just as we were fixing up the door. No chances are taken on putting out fires by hand now.

EXPERIENCES WITH VETERANS.

Naturally I have had some experiences with some of the old fellows who helped to save their country during the war. For a long time I was an easy mark for such of them as were given to absorbing the supply of their needs off others, and there is no use denying that there is occasionally one of that class. All of the clerks in my bailiwic were aware of my friendship for those old fellows and would send the stranded and strapped ones to hunt me up. I don't know that I ever refused to help one along unless I knew he didn't deserve it.

There was one old fellow who was in a habit of getting outside the picket line, at the Soldier's Home pretty frequently, and he would as often fall on me for the loan of a quarter, after the last car toward the home had gone.

"Just a quarter, 'Doc,'" he would say, "to piece me out till morning, for I can't get back to the home to-night. Just a quarter, till my pension comes; then I'll fix it up all right.

The thing got monotonous and I resolved to stop it. The next time he struck me for a quarter, "just to get a bed till morning,' I said to him:

"See here, Mr. Second Division, Sixth Corps, you and I have slept on the ground, down in Johnny Reb land, lots of times, eh?"

"You bet we have, 'Doc,'" said he.

"Well, see here, you just take this note over to Sergeant O'Connor, at the police station, he's good fellow and will give you a bed for the night, dam sight better'n we had next night after Bull Run."

That fellow made a bee line down the street and I never saw him again.

Another whom I recall used to come down and stay with me pleasant nights till I went home in the morning, then he would go home with me, get a good sleep and dinner and in the afternoon I would take him to the home in my buggy. Poor Jack Rowell! He was a good soldier, one of Gen. Braggs Iron Brigade boys. His grave is No. 15 in the Soldiers' Home cemetery and no one is better strewn with flowers on each memorial day, and an American flag and a little red pack, familiar to all First Corps men, are placed at the head of his last bivouac, and I am thus reminded of what his old commander once said:

"Here's to our boyhood, its gold and its gray,
The stars of its winter, the dews of its May;
And when we have ended all earthly joys,
Then, dear Father, take care of the boys."

ONE OF THE BRAVE AND TRUE.

I think it was about fifteen years after the war closed and I had located in Milwaukee that I frequently saw a man in the city whose face and movements seemed familiar to me, but I could not locate him satisfactorily. He would appear every two or three weeks, carrying a grip and going to or from a train. Finally, one night, I stopped him and asked if he had been in the army. He said he had, and was in the Iron Brigade. Yes, he remembered the newsboy of that organization, and right there we renewed old acquaintance, which is sure to remain fresh and often re-renewed while we remain on this side of the shadowy land. That man was Col. J. A. Watrous, one of the bravest men who ever faced a deadly and determined foe and whose heart of kindness goes out in sympathy to all humanity everywhere, a man who has given as much of the best of his life for the benefit of his country and his fellow man as any man ever has, whose loyalty never falters and who never lets an opportunity to do a kindly act pass unimproved. If he should happen to be the last survivor of that great army of loyal and true men whose efforts saved this government from destruction by its foes of bygone days, I believe he would be of all men the most miserable and unhappy, for there would be no one of his comrades in arms left for him to think for, do for, try to make more comfortable and happy than he might otherwise be. Yet all hope he may live thus long.

LEO AND THE DOG.

King Leopold had a namesake in Milwaukee, in fact, quite a number of them, but one in particular I have in mind. He had plenty of cash and did not always fly

Went Out With the Old Year.

low.   A drug store at the corner of Wisconsin and Milwaukee streets was a favorite place with him. That locality was also a general loafing place for a not very valuable dog which nobody seemed to own, but those familiar with him called him George. The dog had become considerable of a nuisance. He had a habit of running into the street and snarling at a passing vehicle, often setting his teeth on a wheel and sometimes would hang on and go around with it during several revolutions.

One New Year's eve the King's namesake concluded

it was time to get rid of that dog. Of course, as the old year passed into Time's big morgue and the young one mounted his pegassus, bells and whistles were tied loose and a bable of noises was on. The conspirators with an abundance of red and blue fire from the drug store door far into the street. As Chief Foley pulled the fire department bell, a signal for all to let 'er go, the drug store door was opened and the dog sent out with a kick and a bundle of tinware securely tied to his tail. He came out with a bound and a yelp, a blaze of red fire on either side of him, and struck a bee line down towards Grand avenue. The bridge tender said he crossed the river at the third tap of the fire bell. Policeman John O'Brien reported him far out on Grand avenue at 12:01 o'clock. The officer at the city limits gave his record there as 12:02, with his nose due west. His record at Wauwatosa was 12:08 and on the road to Oconomowoc. That ended George's loafing at the drug store.

FRITZ AND HIS DOG.

There was once a German tailor known only as Fritz. I think the balance of his name was Kadow. He worked some years for Brenk Bros., when their shop was on Milwaukee street. Fritz was a bachelor, lived by himself in a couple of rooms in the Fourth ward. He had a dog, a sort of a brindle, stub-tailed cur with which he shared his room and his mess. Some of Fritz's remarks to that dog have become current as a story among men. The dog was a lazy whelp and much of the time remained at home loafing in the room. On other days he would go to the shop with Fritz, crawl under his master's bench and sleep the time away between meals, always sharing in the noon lunch. One day when Fritz had taken the smaller end of the lunch he sat on the bench and looked at his dogship in a thoughtful mood. After several minutes reflection he broke out thus:

"You dhink you vas a tog, eh? I dhink so neder. Jah, you vas a tog. I vas Fritz. I vish I vas you und you vas me. Afery tay I vork me hart vile you schleeb.

I git me in the morning up und gooks der breakfast vile
you schleeb. I feeds you und go me to vork und you go
to schleeb. Ad noon I gif you tinner und you go to
schleeb. Ad night I go me home und gooks der subber
und feets you und you go to schleeb, vile I vork me some
more und dhink. Pime py, some tay you go det, dhen I
dakes me my schoffel und tigs in der yart a hole und
puts you in id, und dhat vas der ent of you. Pime py,
some tay agin vit I tie vonce. Dhen what? Dhen I
got to go to hell yet."

There is no certainty but Fritz would have been still
talking to the dog in the same strain had not Casey, the
bookkeeper, who had been listening at the partially open
back door, walked into the shop at that moment.

DOVES FROM SPIRIT LAND.

Time was when I may have been something of a
spiritualist, but I got over it, survived, "passed out"
from under the cloud and am all right now in the rock-
ribbed faith of my earlier years. Years ago, a well-
known spiritualist named Dickenson presented me two
doves, with the injunction to guard them with choicest
care, as they were sacred. According to the story he
had recently been in Boston and while there visited a
materialistic medium, who gave examples of manifesta-
tions. At one of his seances the room was darkened
when two doves flew down at his feet, sent direct from
the spirit world, and these were the ones brought to
Milwaukee and presented to me. I took them home,
gave them the best of care and it nearly broke my heart
when, a few days later they both died, or rather, as the
spiritualists say, "passed out."

A day or two later I met a young nephew of the
noted spiritualist and asked him if he knew anything
about those doves his uncle gave to me. He replied:

"Of course I do. I know all about them. They
were mine before they were yours. One day uncle and
I were down to the German market and I saw a lot of
doves in a box. They belonged to a Polish woman
up in the Eighteenth ward and were for sale. I wanted

a pair of them and uncle said he would buy them for me.
She asked 15 cents apiece for them, but uncle got the
pair for a quarter. I took them home, but soon became
tired of them and he gave them to you. That is all there
is about the doves."

Unless some fakir of the Ethical Society gets up a
seance and causes the spirits of those doves to material-
ize, I shall believe the boy's story rather than his uncle's,
and will take no more stock in Spiritualism, unless it
comes at a discount and through a reliable stock broker.

A PEW SITTING SHOP LIFTER.

In former years it was my custom during holiday
seasons to spend the afternoons in the Chapman store,
on the watch for shoplifters. One day I discovered a
woman in the act of harvesting a fine silk muffler on the
counter and garnering it in her muff. A gentleman now
engaged in real estate business was then floor walker in
that store. I reported the case to him and pointed out
the woman. When approached by him regarding the
matter she promptly surrendered the muffler, claiming
she had picked it up on the floor. I asked him if he did
not intend to prosecute her and he said:

"No, I guess not. She sits in the pew in front of me
at church every Sunday."

HUNGRY FOR LATIN.

When the Pierce block, corner of Wisconsin and Milwaukee streets, was rebuilt, in 1896, there was much
lavishness connected with its equipment. Its owner was
understood to have several barrels of money and didn't
seem to care how he spent it. Among other things he
hired a skilled engineer who was anxious to become a
Latin scholar, and had a mania for drinking wood alcohol. When Ladd & Janssen became settled in the corner store they made a fine window display of various
imported waters, wines and liquors. There was an acro-
batic comedian in town who gave exhibitions at the
shutes and was advertised as hailing from Boston. In

the Third ward, where he lived, he was known as "Jerry from Boston." One night Jerry and the engineer stood in front of the window, when this conversation passed between them:

Engineer—"Jerry, what is the meaning of spirit frumenti, which I saw on a bottle in the store?"

Jerry—"O, that's the best rye whiskey."

Engineer—"What is vini gali?"

Jerry—"What, O, that's peach brandy."

Engineer—"Then what is sic semper tyrannis?"

Jerry—"The best grade of port wine."

Engineer—"I saw a bottle labelled 'Hic Jacet Gloria Mundi.' What's that?"

Jerry—"The best and oldest sherry wine to be found in the world."

The engineer died suddenly a few months later, either from an overdose of wood alcohol or impacted Latin on the brain.

HOW I FOUND GUITEAU.

Probably very few persons now living in Milwaukee are aware that Charles J. Guiteau, the assassin of President Garfield, was ever a resident of this city. He lived here, but, I think, for only a few months.

In November, 1880, one Harold Emmons, a lawyer now residing in Michigan, had his law office in the Marshall block, corner of Wisconsin street and Broadway. His rooms were the same as are now occupied by Col. A. G. Weissert, past commander in Chief of the Grand Army of the Republic. About 1 o'clock, one morning, as I was looking through the building, on my usual round, there was a bright light in Mr. Emmons' room. Such an occurrence was quite a distance from the usual, and I concluded to investigate.

Opening the door I walked in and there was a wiry-built, weazen-faced, snakish-eyed, dark-completed man, apparently of French construction, pacing up and down the back room rehearsing Shakespeare at a rate sufficient to beat a whole band of incipient tragedians preparing for a season of infliction upon a suffering public.

The room pacer appeared considerably excited. He offered me a chair, but said nothing about fumigating, or anything in my particular line, and I excused myself upon the ground that a light in Mr. Emmons' rooms so late at night was rather over the fence from the usual, and I merely wanted to see if everything was all right. He said he had rented desk room there for awhile, and I bid him good night and made my escape.

Next day I met Mr. Emmons and said to him:

"What sort of a French freak have you got in your rooms?"

"O," said he, "I just rented him desk room for a few months, and wish I hadn't. I guess the thing has shipped its rudder. I'll have to get rid of him."

"It wasn't long until the freak was gone from those rooms and I neither saw nor heard of him again until the 2d day of the following July. I came down town in the afternoon and stopped at the T. A. Chapman store when Jake Segar told me Garfield had been assassinated by a fellow named Guiteau.

I remarked that I believed it was the same freak that had desk room in Lawyer Emmons' office, and related my discovery of and short interview with him. I have since corresponded with Sergeant Mason, the man who tried to avenge Garfield's death, and here is a copy of the letter he wrote me:

"Locust Grove, Va., March 18, 1894.

"C. B. Aubery, Milwaukee, Wis. Dear Sir: Your letter of Feb. 23d received. I live on a farm twenty miles from Fredericksburg in Orange county, Va., with my wife and four children; Charles, born Nov. 30, 1880; Lucy, born April 3d, 1885; Will, born Feb. 3d, 1889, and Joseph, born Jan. 4th, 1892.

"I was in the Seventy-eighth Ohio regiment, Second Brigade, Third Division, Seventeenth corps. I was discharged at Indianapolis, Ind., Jan 6, 1865, having served three years. I then enlisted in the regular army at Fredericksburg, Va., July 15, 1866, and served until September 1881. At that time I was First Sergeant of Battery B, Second Artillery. My love and sympathy for Garfield outweighed my military discipline and I sent a bul-

let into his assassin's cell in the hope that I might get
the villain. It was dark and I couldn't see him, yet my
intentions were good enough, so I let it go, hit or miss.
I was tried, got eight years in penitentiary as my sen-
tence, served twenty months and was pardoned.

"Hoping to some time see you and tell you more
than I can write I am

"Yours Truly,
"J. A. Mason."

While on a recent visit to Fredricksburg I tried to
see Mr. Mason, but as he lived twenty miles away and
my time was limited I had to deny myself the pleasure.

HORSELESS MAIL WAGONS.

There isn't many evenings in the year that A. B.
Geilfus doesn't come down town from his home in the

One of Porth's Horseless Wagons.

Seventh ward, walk around a few blocks and then walk
home. He does it for exercise. One night, not long
ago, I met him about 9 o'clock, on Wisconsin street, and
remarked:

"George Porth is right up to date."

"How is that?" he asked.

"Running mail from the postoffice to the railroad
stations with horseless wagons," I replied.

"Well, I declare? Is that so?" asked the water registrar.

"Yes, sure;" said I. "One of the wagons just passed. Didn't you see it?"

"No," said he. "What power does he use? Gasoline engines or electricity?"

"Mules," said I, and his cane just missed my hat.

JOHN AND HIS STAND.

John Bacigalupo,—most everybody knows him only as John—is a scion from Italy who keeps a fruit stand

"And the Flag is Still There."

on the Milwaukee side of the Bunde & Upmeyer store. John and his stand have been there a good many years. Prior to the summer of 1881 his stand was on the corner of the sidewalk, at the store. Then preparations were on for a big reunion of veterans of the war and Mayor T. H. Brown ordered all fruit stands removed from street corners. As I came down town one afternoon John came running to me in great excitement and asked:

"'Doc' what I goin' t' do? Tom Brown he ord plice make tak' stan' off corn'! Don' know what goin' do! Son of gun! He ought get rope an' hang itself!"

I told him I would see; took him in the store and got Mr. Bunde's permission to place his stand against the store, a few feet down from the corner, if John would keep an American flag on the stand. There have been few days when the flag was not there and John has voted the Republican ticket ever since.

ROBBERS AND BURGLARS CAUGHT.

About 2 o'clock one morning in March, 1885, there was a highway robbery on Michigan street, between Broadway and Milwaukee street. Three toughs held up a man named McLaughlin. The robbers were John Long, John Kirk and Henry Woods. Policeman David Harris, now a guard at Waupun, and John I. Murphy, were close after the robbers. I was near the front of the Bunde & Upmeyer store when the three fellows came up Jefferson street and crossed to the alley now by the Hotel Pfister and stepped back in the shade of a building. Harris and Murphy came up Wisconsin street in search of them. I pointed out their game and told them to stand where they were and I would chase the robbers out. Crossing over by the postoffice I then crossed Milwaukee street and went through a hall, coming out on the alley a few rods north of the robbers. I got pretty close to them and ordered them to put up their hands. They all ran and I fired several shots over their heads. By the description I got of them Woods and Kirk were captured the next day. Long left the city and was never captured. A couple of years later he fell off a steamer in the Mississippi river and drowned. Kirk got a year and six months in the house of correction and Woods got two years in Waupun.

About 2 o'clock in the morning, Dec. 13, 1875, D. C. Reed, then government boiler inspector, came up Jefferson street, turned down Wisconsin and met me in front of Stark Bros.' store. About two rods behind him came Pat Donahue, one of the toughest products of the Third ward. Mr. Reed stopped me and as Pat came up said: "'Doc.' this fellow has just robbed the Troy laundry. I saw him in there."

I knew Pat was desperate and would shoot if necessary, so I made a play to take his part, remarking: "O, I know him. He wouldn't do such a thing as that."

Mr. Reed insisted that he was right and he and Pat began arguing the case. As they became interested I tripped Pat's feet from under him, laid him on his back and dropped upon him. He reached for his revolver. I caught his hands, asked Reed to hold one while I held the other and blew my whistle for the regular policeman, Michael O'Connor, now lieutenant of police. He was there in a minute and Pat went in. He got six months in the House of Correction. Four years ago he was found dead in a freight car in the C. M. & St. P. yard.

One night in the fall of 1878 I discovered a fellow in the alley at the rear of the store now occupied by William Reckmeyer. I had forgotten my revolver, but had a big duplex whistle in my pocket. I pulled it upon him. He threw up his hands and I marched him out to the street. Just then Michael Peck, the regular officer, came along, identified my prisoner, gave him a certificate of good character and we discharged him. It was a false alarm, but it has always been my policy to take no chances of letting a possible burglar escape.

SOMETHING OF A STORM.

During my twenty-five years out nights I have seen some storms. One night I was knocked down by lightning in front of the Chapman store. I managed to get to the Windsor hotel. Officer Michael Peck happened to be there. He hastened some restoratives into me and went out to investigate. The lightning had struck a house just south of where the Goldsmith building now stands and ran down a lightning rod to the ground. A policeman was also knocked down by the shock a block farther away.

That was a night when the wind blew. There was an oak barrel in front of Dan. Jones' store. The wind blew the staves and hoops away, leaving only the bung-hole. Gray Bros. had just drilled an artesian well at the

Colby & Abbott building. The wind blew that well out by the roots, turned it inside out and dropped it away up the river near the flushing tunnel. It took a week to get it back and drive it into its hole again. This story ought to be correct. It is just as I received it the next day.

NIGHTS OFF DUTY.

During my twenty-five years of service as special night police I can safely say I have not had twenty-five nights off duty, and those have generally been during Grand Army events, and a couple of other times. During one of the latter, I was helping entertain a friend who was attending a Masonic event. He is a Janesville business man. In 1862 he was a member of "Jeb." Stuart's black horse rebel cavalry and had the honor of capturing me and sending me off to Richmond to become acquainted with Libby prison. That night was spent differently from my nights in Libby prison.

Another night off which I recall was the first one after McKinley's election to the presidency. As I came down for duty I saw trouble ahead. Mel. Sanford was beginning to receive returns by private wire. Operator Sam. Illers was at the ticking machine and John M. Ewing was already shouting in the enthusiastic flush of victory won. In the Pfister all were in high glee, with John M. in the lead. I put a substitute on my beat, put in the night with the other victors and finally went home about the same as the others did—full, of the satisfaction that prosperity had struck us.

A SUSPICIOUS CHARACTER.

Away back in the olden time a stranger came to town and located on the second floor at 116 Milwaukee street. He wore a flashy tie ornamented with a silver quarter made into a pin with a picture of the sun engraved upon it. I frequently saw him standing in the hall door and was a trifle suspicious of him. At that time Col. E. A. Calkins was running a Sunday newspaper in that building. One hot night I caught the facetious Colonel out barefooted gathering items for his paper and asked him who the stranger was. He replied:

"O, he's all right. That's George Peck and he's going to run a newspaper up there in a room next to mine."

I believe I never told George how near I came to running him in on suspicion.

SCARCITY OF FIRES AND CRIMES.

Aside from the burning of the Chapman store there have been few fires of consequence on my beat in twenty-five years. During Chief Foley's long reign at the head of the fire department he has given me many valuable pointers on watching for fires, always insisting that any number of false alarms, when there was probability of a fire, were preferable to even brief delay in time of danger. His constant vigilance, in that respect has been a blessing to the city.

In this connection I am surely justified in referring to the persistent efforts of Chief of Police Janssen in maintaining order. He has never once failed to give me encouragement and assistance when needed. I could relate many instances in which his foresight and wise direction have undoubtedly averted the perpetration of crime, and there are doubtless many more night watchmen in the city who could give similar testimonials to his efficiency.

LANDMARKS SPARED BY TIME.

Time has wrought its changes rapidly during twenty-five years. Hundreds of the olden-time familiar faces have passed away. Yet some remain. The largest group now to be found in one establishment on my beat, who were there twenty-five years ago, are in the Chapman store, where they have grown up and some of them have grown gray in the service. Those who have passed the entire quarter of a century there and are still on duty are Manager P. R. Hannifin, J. A. Seger, Harry C.

Barber, B. V. Seger, John Muller, Hugo Bohn, A. Arnstein, W. H. Crossman, Miss Lottie Davis, Augustus Chapman, B. Koepke, Matt. Wagner, Martin Muer, G. C. Murphy and Harry Lawrence, and "Billy" Ormsby, many years a favorite with Mr. Chapman, is still in the service of the Chapman family.

At Herman Heyn's store there is but one of the old time attaches, a young lady who modestly requests me not to print her name. Louis W. Bunde, of Bunde & Upmeyer, was a cash boy in the Chapman store; so was that firm's optician, Henry Waldie. Otto Zedler, also now with Bunde & Upmeyer, was with the old time firm of Stanley & Camp. Mr. Keogh, of Carroll & Keogh, was a clerk in the T. A. Chapman store and Louis Tisdale, secretary of the Stark Bros. Company, was Stark Bros.' bookkeeper then.

One old-time friend I miss, but often recall one of his favorite expressions. He was Edward Stark. Parting one night, after a chat on the corner near the store, he said: "Well, 'Doc.' good night; keep a good lookout, for

> "When the iron tongue of Time
> Tolls the hour of midnight,
> How often we say 'Time flies.'
> When 'tis not time that flies,
> But we who are passing away."

In those days agone, Mark Tyson, who rode his mare up the full flight of stairs into the Newhall house bar-room, took a drink and treated the crowd on a hundred dollar bet, was among the active and conspicuous. William Sexton was among the leading boomers when there was sport in sight and G. W. Featherstonhaugh, now relegated into the shades of comparative obscurity, was a conspicuous figure. He was a member of the second constitutional convention, which adopted the State Constitution, and was credited with having written most of that document. Featherstonhaugh was one of the bright men of that period and capable of saying as mean things as any. The latter faculty he retained well, as a couple of instances will illustrate.

Some ten to fifteen years ago he was passing along Milwaukee street when a young man whose front name was Byron was sitting on a bench in front of his father's place of business. As if to clear his throat he gave a couple of semi-coughs. Instantly Featherstonhaugh turned upon him with:

"Young man, what do you mean, sir? You, sir, named after an illustrious poet and only the son of a botch painter, sir!" and the old man went his way.

Not long after the great telegraph operators' strike, along about 1885, Peter McGill was sitting in front of a hotel when Mr. Featherstonhaugh approached him and remarked:

"Young man, you are a Scotchman, aren't you?"

"I plead guilty to the charge, sir," said the gentlemanly Peter.

"The Scotch are a sturdy race of strong and able men, sir. Do you happen to have a spare quarter about you?"

"I have, sir," said Peter, handing him the desired assurance of two drinks.

"But, sir, the dirty cusses are all lousy, have the itch, and the Duke of Argyle had a post set up on which to scratch his lousy back," was the old man's instant rejoinder as the quarter slipped into his hand, and he moved along.

Among those seen regularly around my beat twenty-five years ago and who are still here are Judge H. L. Palmer, Judges Mallory and Jenkins, the venerable William E. Cramer, A. J. Aikens, the Vermont Yankee; Edward and John F. Cramer, Herman, Julius, Louis and Adolph Bleyer, all of the Evening Wisconsin; Henry and Albert Bleyer, of the Sentinel; Frank and William Bigelow, Charles Pfister, Drs. Leustrom, Mason, Carlson, Ladd, Marks, Wolcott and Bartlett; E. O. Ladd, B. M. Weil, Herman Heyn, C. J. and Joshua Stark, H. N. Hempsted, Rufus Allen, George Eddy, A. G. Weissert, Louis Auer, Fred S. Ilsley, C. A. Higgins, Capt. C. J. Sackett, Senator John L. Mitchell, James Bryden, Alexander Cochran, Robert Eliot, E. P. Bacon, W. J. Curtin, A. G. Rose, Edward Pyatt, now of Chicago; E. C. Wall, Charles Whitnall, John Johnston, Commodore W. H. Wolf, Gregory Hurson, Frank L. Vance, Albert Huegin,

M. P. Walsh, Ed. Keogh, John J. Crilly, I. G. Mann, James Graham, James Bannen, Sr.; E. P., A. R. and Q. A. Matthews, Peter Van Vechten, Henry Fink, H. C. Koch, Julius Lasche, Col. Thomas Keer, Col. Jerome Johnson, W. C. Swain, Sam. Tate, A. G. Wright, Daniel Wells, Jr.; Samuel Marshall, Charles Ilsley, Henry C. Payne, Henry Bracken. W. J. Denny, Herman A. Bierwald, Harry M. Allen. Charles Whitnall, John Campbell, A. J. W. Pierce, James Conroy, Joseph Lyon, Henry Fess, Pat. O'Brien, the Evening Wisconsin pressman during the last thousand years; George Phipps, Jonathan Magie, Aliton Streeter, Sam. F. Peacock, Prof. A. G. Faville, A. W. Rich, Louis Silber, Charles Munkwitz, Col. Cornelius Wheeler, David Adler, Edgar W. Colman, Maj. Joseph Oliver, I. M. Lederer, Ed. Silverman, Hiram J. Mabbett, James Fowler, George Howard, Louis W. Bunde, William H. Upmeyer, Norman L. Burdick, Thomas H. Brown, Capt. Edward Ferguson, John S. George, Dr. Lytton Flinn, Peter Frattinger, D. H., Albert and Dr. S. H. Friend, Carl Landsee, Colin Campbell, Jabez Smith, Robert C. Spencer, Charles H. Saveland, Henry Riemers, John Roper, E. E. Chapin, Eugene S. Elliott, Edward Gray, Michael Dunn, Daniel Kennedy, Edward Sivyer, Edward McCann, Col. Florian J. Ries, W. T. Durand, Samuel R. Bell, Patsey Coin, James Hannan, John Hannan, Capt. A. B. Davis, Maj. A. Ross Houston, Joe and Arthur Gressing, F. M. Keats, William F. Zeltner, James W. Campbell and William H. Partridge, shoe dealers, Henry Reilly, George I. Robinson, Charles and Frank Anson, Jonah Williams, E. P. Hackett, Thomas Ramsey, Charles W. Hamilton, A. K. Camp, Henry Ramsey, John Hinton, Ferdinand Pripps, who was janitor of the Evening Wisconsin building when the famous spring in the basement was conspicuous; and an old time drug clerk known as "Prof. Parbelow." And I suppose a lot more of names will come to me when this is in print and make me mad at myself for not having mentioned them.

DAN SHEHAN'S EXPERIENCES.

Dan Shehan lived in the Third ward. He was then roundsman on the police force, ex-patrolman, ex-detective and an all around politician, either Republican or Democrat, according to the crowd he was with. Dan never drank but was an inveterate smoker. A friend once asked him to take a drink.

"No, Oi'll not drink, but Oi'll take a cigar," said Dan.

"Yes, give Dan a good ten cent cigar," said his friend.

"Oi'll not take a tin cinter, but Oi'll take two foives," said Dan.

One day, when on the force, Dan was sent out on the West side to investigate a reported burglary. Entering the house, with hat in hand, in response to an invitation by the lady of the house, to come in, this conversation followed:

Dan.—"Is this Mrs. S———?"

Mrs. S.—"Yes, sir; what do you want?

Dan.—"Sure, mem, Oi was sint here by the chafe to ax yez was it at the front or rare door av yer house that the burglars intered."

Mrs. S.—"It was neither, sir. It appears that the burglar came in and went out again through a side window."

Dan.—"Sure, mem, if that be the case I do be thinkin' he was a shlippery chap an' it will be afther takin' the whole foorce to bag him, begorry."

One time Dan's beat was in the Seventh ward. He was anxious to know how the people on the beat esteemed him and meeting a little girl he accosted her:

"Shay, sissy, did yez iver be hearin' yer mother sayin' ony thing about me?"

"Yes, she says you are a nigeramus," was the little one's prompt reply.

That afternoon I met Dan, and in a semi-confidential tone he said:

"Misther Ahbry, wud yez moind tellin' me phat's the manin' av the worrud 'nigeramus?'"

"That's a man born just as other men are, but possessed of superior qualifications in one way or another which the more they are cultivated the more conspicuous they become," said I.

"Thank ye surr," said Dan, "Oi raleized thot it wuz a terrum ixprissin' and bortherin' on some degra av supariority. Wud yez coom over and take a segair wid me?"

Alderman Shaughnessy once perpetrated a joke on Dan. The alderman attended a meeting at the bishop's hall. It was a very rainy night. One of Dan's daughter's was at the meeting. It was at the time Dan was rounds-man. On account of the rain the alderman offered to escort Dan's daughter home with the protection of his umbrella. Arriving at the house he looked through the window and saw Dan stretched upon the lounge asleep, instead of being out looking after the men in his charge. As he parted from the young woman he said:

"Should any one ask who escorted you home say it was Henry Miles."

Miles was a patrolman on a beat in the Seventh ward, and the alderman had a suspicion Dan would ques-tion the daughter as to her escort.

"Daughter, who kem home wid yez?" asked Dan.

"It was Henry Miles, father," said she.

"Arrah! It was, eh?" said Dan as he climbed off the lounge and slid his arms down through his suspenders. "Begobs, Oi'll be seein' about thot," and he got into his coat, hoisted an umbrella and shot into the darkness and the down pour of sky juice.

After a hunt of an hour he found Miles pacing his beat with the faithfulness of a veteran before the gates of a doomed city.

"Where wuz yez, Henry Miles, at 11:30 o'clock?" de-manded Dan.

"After a moment's thought Miles replied:

"At the Court House park, sir."

"Indade ve wur not, Henry Miles. Let yez be moindin' yer bate now till morning. Sure Oi do be knowin' where yez wuz and the chafe'll know it in the mornin'."

The alderman took occasion to put the chief onto

the job before Dan got around in the morning, and when
Dan came around the chief said to him:

"Mr. Shehan, where were you about 11:30 o'clock
last night?"

"Sure, sir," said Dan, "Oi think that wuz about the
toime I wuz on Henry Mileses bate in the Siventh ward."

"Yes, but about half an hour before you were up to
see Henry?" said the chief.

"O, yis, Oi see, dhat was whin Oi wint down till the
house to lave off me wit clothes and put on some dry
ones," said Dan.

"All right, Mr. Shehan, keep an eye to your men
during the night," said the chief, and Dan never knew
how the game was played upon him.

A TRAMP PRINTER'S STORY.

About 2 o'clock one summer morning back in 1875,
a genius, ripe in years, abundant in experience, thoroughly schooled in that wisdom which comes through
observation, and, apparently, an all around philosopher,
came my way. He came leisurely up the street, as one
weary from long journeying in the good, old, natural
way. That was a year during which the country seemed
alive with tramp printers, as a rule, men who would do
no harm, being generally possessed of that reasonable
order of good sense and reason which sits side by side
on the throne with fair education. In short, men who
know somthing and think. It was my experience that
at least nine of every ten tramp printers would ask for
work the first thing they did. However hungry or tired
they might be, they were possessed of an ambition to
earn the needs of life. Of course there were exceptions
to this rule, but they were rare. A tramp-printer usually
spent his own money, whether it was for bread or for
booze.

As my genius approached I spotted him for one of
the craft and accosted him with:

"Good morning."

"Good morning, sir; and a nice, balmy morning it
is, too; a morning worth living in and the kind which,

as a rule, sir, only God's unfortunates have opportunity to participate in the glories of."

"Gee whiz," said I to myself as he rattled off his brief oration, "here's a corker. Guess I'll pump him a little; may get something good. 'Where goin'?'"

"That is just the piece or information I am seeking, sir," said he, "and I'll be greatly obliged to you for it. My ambition at this moment is to get into a good bed for the space of about four hours, but as I know that is not only the unexpected, which is not likely to happen just now, but also practically the impossible, I'll be greatly obliged if you will tell me where I can be permitted to lie down on a board and rest secure until the regular working hour, when I hope to find a few hours' work in some one of the daily newspaper offices, enough at least to earn a bite of breakfast."

"Owl right," said I, "I'll show you where," and as we started towards the station where he would merely be booked as a lodger and given the best opportunity that place offered for the desired rest, I asked:

"Where d'ye live?"

"Kind sir," said he, "you mistake me. I don't happen to be one of those favored mortals who live, except in a figurative sense. As the poet has said:

> " 'Here in this body spent
> I stay and strive and roam
> And nightly pitch my moving tent
> A day's march nearer home.' "

There was an all night restaurant on our route and I walked the old fellow into it, motioned him to a chair and sat down opposite him at the table, remarking to the clerk "Two coffees, sandwiches and a pie."

My genius looked puzzled for a moment, then arose and looking me straight in the eye said:

"If it is all the same to you, my friend, I will wait while you take your lunch, but, to tell you the truth, I haven't the price, and it is a rule with me to earn before I eat."

"Now, see here, my Covey," said I, showing my star, "you are in my hands and, 'by the great Jehovah and the Continental Congress,' you've no right to decline to be my guest. You're going to eat a bite, and I'll bet on it."

"If you really insist upon it," said he, "but it is against my principle to eat before I earn."

I insisted and he held the chair down again.

"That Ethan Allen quotation sounded familiar to me, sir," said he, "I've heard my grandfather make use of it many times. He was in company with the old patriot when he made the remark and carried his point in the cause of liberty and freedom of conscience."

"You've had a lot of experience in your time," I suggested.

"Yes, some, sir;" said he. "I have seen considerable, tried to observe pretty carefully and form my own conclusions. I have seen much to admire and some to abhor. This is called a strange world, sir, but it is not, as I view it. The world is all right. There is a divine and gracious arrangement of all things in it, as the good Lord designed them, and some queer people, besides, sir. By the way, sir, I venture to say you are not much of a church man."

I had a suspicion that the old fellow had a store of good things in his head, if I could get him to unwinding. He ate like a thorough gentleman of culture and I was studying a way to touch a key that would set him going more freely. I ordered second cups of coffee and rather demurely confessed that I was not over active in the matter of church going, and that perhaps I ought to be more attentive to matters of religion, and asked why he formed the conclusion just expressed. That query proved the hit I was looking for. His face brightened and clouded alternately during fully half a minute before he spoke, then he leaned back in the chair and said:

"Because, sir, I discovered that you gave more thought to feeding the hungry at your side than to converting the heathen thousands of miles away. I venture the further assertion, sir, that you would not contribute a nickel for the heathen of India or Africa or any other foreign land, so long as there was want in your own land. And I believe that principle involves the true spirit of religion. I am not wholly an unbeliever, sir. I believe in God and the Saviour, but I take no stock in modern practices called religion. Why, sir, this very year missionary organizations in this country have sent thousands of dollars to the heathen in far off countries, while thousands of people are starving in the great cities of our own country. They hold missionary meeting in palatial meeting houses, whose spires pierce the clouds with golden tipped fingers, and beg contributions for the heathen, with the poor, almost naked and starving at their very doors. They array themselves in silks and do their devotions in cushioned pews, before high salaried priests, and the burden of their prayers is for the salvation of the heathen who would steal the throne of heaven if they were in there and could get away with it. They give no thought to the suffering at home, but burden their poor souls with anguish over supposed misery thousands of miles beyond their sight. As I said before, I am a believer in religion, sir, but not in the kind much in practice. It don't seem to me much like the Saviour, who preached the gospel of humanity to the multitudes on the streets, broke bread with the poorest of the poor and was without a place to lay his head at night."

We had finished the lunch and I accompanied the old man to the station, fixed him the best bunk possible and told him to go in the morning to a certain printing office and ask for the foreman whose name I gave him on a slip of paper. Then I went my round, went to the office I had named, unlocked the door, went in and left a sealed note on Foreman George Eddy's desk. The old man got steady work for nearly two months. He was a superior workman for those times and when he left town he did not have to walk or go hungry.

THE OLD, OLD SAFE.

One evening in the spring of 1883, George Cooley, now dead, George Eddy and myself, during a half hour chat in front of the Chapman store, conceived the idea of raising a fund for a Soldiers' monument. Out of it grew the Soldiers' Monument association, of which I am a member. The same summer the old safe which stood until recently in front of the postoffice, as a contribution box for the monument fund, was given to me for that purpose by A. D. Seaman, and hauled and placed in position by Deacon Edwin Hyde. It had been through three fires and was of little value. The key was placed in the hands of Frank G. Bigelow and the safe was occasionally opened, its contents taken out and credited to the fund. A few months ago I broke it open, one morning just at daylight, and robbed it, getting $12.19, which I shall turn over to the original monument fund. The newspapers made a sensation of the robbery. The safe was artistically painted by Jonah Williams, when first placed in position, but it finally became rusty and is now in a scrap iron pile.

IN THE WRONG LODGE.

One of the worst frightened men I have met on my beat in twenty-five years was F. C. Wieben, a barber up in the First ward. Not very long ago he came down town on a wrong night to attend a meeting of the Barber's union. He went to the customary hall, gave the raps and password and was admitted. Imagine his surprise at finding himself surounded by such men as Peter Van Vechten, Louis Lachman, Capt. Norton, Samuel Harper and others of that set. He knew they were not barbers, and was not long in discovering that he had gotten into a meeting of the Patriarchial Circle. With awe striking solemnity he was surrounded by dignitaries of that order and was led to believe a most horrible fate was the penalty of his intrusion. When permitted to escape with his life he promptly came to me and begged to be guarded to his home lest the infuriated Patriarchs should follow and waylay him. He will not mistake the night of the barbers' meeting again in a hurry.

SOME OLD-TIME FIRMS.

Among good fellows who engaged in business on my beat, in my early days as watchman, are George and Arthur Wright, in the drug store they still occupy at the post office alley. Among their early employes who are still with them were Sol. Eckstein, Ned Krauskopf and Harry Pierce, all royal good fellows and widely known. All have served their time as night watch sleeping in the store, though none of them ever liked the job, especially in the earlier years, because of the presence of so many cats around the alley back of the Leigh house, and the horseless wagons at the post office, which were constant sources of annoyance.

This reliable old drug house has graduated some good druggists, among them Thomas Ladd, of the drug firm of Ladd & Janssen, at the corner of Wisconsin and Milwaukee streets, and Daniel Jones, in business for himself a few doors farther up Milwaukee street.

Another old time firm is the T. S. Gray Company, the popular book store firm, nearly all of the years in their present quarters.

Then there is the firm of Campbell & Partridge, shoe dealers, nearly a quarter of a century in business on Wisconsin street.

Herman Heyn is, I believe, the only other one in business in the immediate vicinity who was there even twenty years ago.

A HARDY HIGHLANDER.

About eight years ago a company of Scotchmen were up from Chicago to attend the St. Andrew's society picnic. After the fun of the day and night they went to the Windsor hotel and were given rooms on the third floor. During the night one fellow in the party by the name of Cameron got to fooling around the open window and fell out. He went down through a skylight, the glass of which was an inch in thickness and landed on a broad shelf in the Evening Wisconsin job printing room. After a long hunt I found him there, mutilated, bleeded and groaning. The patrol wagon was called and took him to the police station where a botch surgeon plastered up his wounds. Early in the morning the report went out that Cameron had been killed. Peter McGill was secretary of the society and he, with other Scotchmen hastened to the hotel to view the remains.

But Cameron refused to remain dead. Well done up in court plaster he was down at the Chamber of Commerce seeing the sights. He has attended the annual picnic every year since and says he will keep training and coming until he can jump back up where he fell down.

THE NEWHALL FIRE.

I have omitted saying anything about the burning of the Newhall house, on the morning of Jan. 10, 1883. I do not want to say anything about it now. It is not pleasant to turn to that page of memory, no trace upon which can bring aught but sorrow. May or June, with all the forces of nature full of life, and promise, and beauty, are pleasanter than December, in this rigid, northern climate, with all the beauties of nature in the cold clasp of winter's death and dreariness.

I would rather devote a whole book to thoughts and events which would produce none other than pleasant thoughts and cheerful memories than one line to that which could yield only saddened thoughts and awaken only bitter memories.

I have seen the horrors of rebel prison pen, the carnage of battle with its awful destruction of human life and the devastation following in its wake, but they form no basis for comparison with the horrors resulting from that fire, with its twenty-eight identified and thirty-six unidentified dead. I could record pages of incidents connected with the event, but they would serve only to awaken sad memories. I mention it only that the date may be again recorded and as one of the events happening during my twenty-five years as night watchman on the streets of Milwaukee.

WALKING AROUND A BLOCK.

Not very long ago a young blood of the Seventh ward, whom I will call Charley, because that is what his parents call him, came around on my beat pretty late in the night, with an immense load on. I tried to in-

duce him to go to a hotel and go to bed, urging him not
to go home with that jag. He flatly refused to go to
bed. Then I urged him to walk around a block a few
times and wear it off. He agreed to that and started.
He was as good as his word and reported to me at every
round, though he occasionally dropped off to inquire
when "Mel." Sanford's next quarterly birthday was due.
Daylight found him still tramping around that block.
Then he said he had been around the block three times
and was sober enough to go home. As a matter of fact
he had been around the block just forty-two times.

NEWSBOY IN THE ARMY.

A friend of mine said to me: "'Doc,' I hear you are
writing a book."

"Yes, trying to," said I.

"Well, don't forget to give us a touch of your experiences as newsboy in the army," said he. And he exacted
a promise to that effect.

I wish I had not made that promise. If I had fully
realized that to fulfill it I would have to write about myself and my own doings, I would not have made it, and
will now only say enough to redeem it.

When President Lincoln called for volunteers to help
put down the rebellion, in the spring of 1861, my four
brothers enlisted. I was a barefooted lad thirteen years
old. They entered the Second Vermont regiment which
left Burlington, Vt., for the front, June 21, 1861. As the
train bearing the regiment away was moving out of the
old Burlington depot, I jumped on and kept out of sight
of my brothers until we reached New York. Then they
discovered me and telegraphed mother that I was with
them and all right. An uncle supplied me with shoes and
some clothing, and I reached Washington with the regiment. While in camp there I worked for Lieut. C. K.
Leach, taking care of his quarters, earning two dollars
a week. When the regiment went to the front I went
with it, doing all kinds of jobs for the boys and finally
went to selling newspapers. In due time I got a horse
with which to go to the base of supplies for my news-

papers. After the first battle of Bull Run the army was
camped at Arlington Heights for the winter. Then I
launched out into the newspaper business. I discovered
that the Wisconsin men were extensive readers of newspapers and nourished their acquaintance. I stuck by
McClellan's army during the campaign of 1862 and kept
up the newspaper business. Nov. 10, 1862, I left camp
for Washington to get my supply of papers. It was
thirty-one miles to Washington and "Jeb." Stuart's black
horse rebel cavalry was making things interesting in that
region of country. I got my supplies and left Washing-

As Newsboy in the Army.

ton in the morning of Nov. 11. During my absence the
army started on the move. About noon, Nov. 12, I was
leaving New Baltimore, supposing I would soon be
within the Union lines. But, instead I was soon a prisoner of war and the rebels confiscated my horse and supplies. One of my first acquaintances while a prisoner
was Horace Baker, of the Twelfth Massachusetts regiment, also a prisoner. Next day we, with about fifty
other prisoners were marched to Gordonsville where
we were placed in freight cars, shipped to Richmond and placed in Libby prison. Sunday morn-

ing. Dec. 12, I, with a lot more, was paroled and sent
to City Point, then to Annapolis where the soldiers went
into camp and I was told I could go where I pleased.

I had $380 in greenbacks, which Maj. Thomas P.
Turner, keeper of Libby prison, had taken care of during
my imprisonment and returned to me when I left. I
took the first train for Washington, got myself cleaned

Filling Canteens for the Boys.

up, learned that the Iron Brigade was at Belleplain Land-
ing, got a supply of papers and started for that point. I
was welcomed back and went at once to selling papers
again. I stuck to the Iron Brigade to the finish, was
with it in all of its campaigning and supplied it with newspapers to the best of my ability. I was in Washington
after papers when the war closed, was in Ford's theatre
when President Lincoln was assassinated, came to Wisconsin in the wake of its Iron Brigade regiments, have
been here ever since and here I am now. I could fill
several such books as this with incidents of the war and
the Iron Brigade, but this is not a war history.

I was invited to attend the monument dedication at
Gettysburg, and there met many I had known in the
army. On a trip south recently I met the men who captured me, and we became warm friends. My best pleasure is in attending reunions of the Iron Brigade and
living war time days over again.

A friend of mine once said it would be impossible for

me to write a column or talk half an hour without referring to the war. I guess that is so, but I have tried to
avoid my weakness in this book. Yet out of my collection of war relics I want to give one short paper, because
it will be of interest to Wisconsin veterans. The paper

Libby Prison.

was given me by a friend, to add to my collection, under
promise that I would not print a long list of names which
he said were those of officers and men who ran away
from the battle at Antietam. Here is the letter:

"Headquarters, Fort Terrell, Mumfordsville, Ky.,
Nov. 28, 1863.

"Maj.-Gen. U. S. Grant, Commanding Department of
the Mississippi.

"Dear Sir:—I respectfully request a position on your
staff as aid de camp. To desire to be connected with a
man so distinguished as yourself is not only natural but
patriotic. I send no recommendations, as I have enough
on file in the department of the Cumberland. My superior
officers here are strangers to me and I have my own private reasons for the request. My military experience is
limited to Perryville and Stone River and the example of
the illustrious and the honorable dead. Lieut.-Col. S. W.
B——, of the Eighteenth Wisconsin, formerly and now of
the Veteran Reserve Corps, is my mother's father. The
appointment would be a particular favor to him. I have
the honor, General, to refer you to Gen. C. S. Stark-
weather, Col. G. Bingham or any Wisconsin officers

who know me. I have the honor to be, General, very respectfully, your obedient servant, etc., etc., etc.

On the reverse side of the letter is the following: "Hd. Qrs. Mil. Div. Miss., In the Field, Chattanooga, Tenn., Dec. 11th, 1863. Respectfully returned. There is no vacancy at present on the staff of the general commanding.   "By order of Maj.-Gen. Grant,
                    "Geo. K. Leet, A. A. G."

Ridiculous as this may seem, it is a true copy of the letter in my possession, minus names. The writer of the letter was probably as much entitled to the position he sought as I am to consideration as a Union veteran, yet when the governor of the great state of Vermont says, "Give my compliments to 'Doc' Aubery, who was a Vermont soldier," that settles it and my chance for a pension is all right.

Before and After My Stay in Libby Prison.

ONE ON A FISHERMAN.

One good fellow, now dead, was a favorite with all night men. His long suit was fishing. He used to go with "the boys" out to Pewaukee lake Sundays and, whether the others caught any fish or not he would come back in the evening and slip up a side street with a nice string of bass, always managing to let some reporter see him.

Next day after one of his trips a letter came for him

from an old fisherman at Pewaukee, and there was a bill in the letter—for fish, of course. Then his snap was out. In some way a reporter got on to the matter and the whole game was published. Of course the exposure was laid to "that dam 'Doc'," and the fisherman and his friends swore to get even with me.

They fitted up a dummy at a rear window of a store,

which had every appearance of a burglar just going to enter the store. I watched the proceeding from the corner of another building and overheard the chuckling over the anticipated fun they were to have when I would begin to shoot and yell for police. When the thing was all fixed they went around the corner to see a man and get into another back room where they could hear the fun when trouble would begin.

As they moved away I stole up, cut the string, carried the dummy away and put it in the Evening Wisconsin engine room. Next morning it was hanging at a prominent corner and labeled, "A Pewaukee Fisherman."

PLEASANT TO REMEMBER.

I shall not soon forget my first meeting with Capt. Charles King, at Chain Bridge, Va. It was a pleasant meeting, just such as thousands of other persons have had with him in the army and elsewhere. It is always a pleasure to meet such broad-minded, thorough gentlemen as he is.

SOME BOOK BINDERY LIES.

A few years ago I had some volumes of magazines I wanted bound and took them down to one of the binderies. The manager said I could get them in about two weeks. I went back at the end of a month as my wife was anxious for the books. They were not ready but I was told they were in the hands of the stitchers and would be finished in a week.

Looking over in a corner I saw my bundle of magazines with my name on the package.

"Are you quite sure my magazines are being stitched?" I asked.

"Yes, dead sure," was the reply. "I carried the bundle to the girls myself one day last week and told them to hurry them up."

"Guess you must be mistaken," said I, "for that stack

OF MILWAUKEE AFTER DARK

over there in the corner looks very much like mine."

He looked at it, saw he was caught, flushed a little and said:

"No, that's not yours; those belong to 'Doc.' Aubery. He just brought them in a few days ago."

"That is just what I thought," said I, "only it was a month ago that I brought the bundle here."

"What! Are you Aubery?" said the skillful prevaricator. "I thought you were Hexamer. Then it is Hexamer's job I am rushing through. Well, I'll get right at yours this afternoon."

It ran on about six months and I hadn't got my books yet, but had considerable fun over that bookbinder's explanations of the delay, well knowing he was handling a decidedly elastic kind of truth. During the time I discovered that other persons were also meeting with disappointments of the same kind and learned from some of the workmen in the bindery that magazine binding suffered constant delay because of the rush of new work for important business houses, of which the bindery had a large run. But I got handsomely avenged.

One day a couple of weeks before Christmas I went to the bindery to see how my work was progressing when in came a bright eyed young woman who, stepping up to the boss, said:

"Mr. ———, when is that book of mine going to be bound? I am very anxious to have it done for a Christmas present to my mother."

"It will be done day after to-morrow, sure," said he. "It is all bound and in the drying press now. I'll send it up to the house day after to-morrow, without fail."

"Now, you are quite sure you will not disappoint me this time?" queried the fair visitor.

"O, dead sure. Bet your life on it. If it were really necessary I could send it up to-morrow, but it will be better to dry a day longer."

"Now, look here, Mr. ———," said she, "I haven't any book here to be bound, nor did I ever have one here. I just wanted to see how big a string of them you could tell at a single sitting."

She then left the bindery. I did likewise, but I never

knew whether the boss of that shop suspected anybody of setting up that job on him.

OYSTERS AND THEIR HABITS.

Here is one which isn't entirely new. Like some other things, it has been used a little, but it is just as good as new, for it has never before been told correctly. The idea, or maybe, the fact in it has been printed a couple or two times, to suit different occasions. But it actually happened in Milwaukee.

There was a house within a short stone's throw of the site of the new government building. After having long served the purpose of a residence it was used as a club house before it went up into the eighteenth ward on wheelbarrows propelled by Polish women.

One Thanksgiving night the club then occupying it had a banquet. A prominent caterer supplied the feast which included a long list of good things, besides a large bucket of raw oysters. The bivalves were generously partaken of by all the party except one, a scientist and analytical chemist, who persistently declined them. Every one wanted to know why he wouldn't eat oysters and he promised to tell them later on.

As quite a number of my employers were participants at the feast, a colored waiter was sent out to hunt me up and bid me come and eat and drink. I promised to call in later, after the drug stores were closed up, and about midnight ushered myself in. There was yet an abundance of solid food and the liquid was going around pretty freely. I was seated near the chemist, who was my personal friend, and a waiter brought me a big plate of raw oysters. The chemist gave me a sharp look and shook his head. I declined the oysters and proceeded to avenge myself on roast turkey, sandwiches and a couple of tanks of liquid. It appeared that I was filling up according to the identical program followed by the chemist, at which some one remarked:

"There is another crank on oysters."

Then the whole party demanded the chemist's explanation of why he refused to eat oysters, and they got it. He said:

"Gentlemen, if you had analized as many oysters as I have, and understood what the analyses tell, you would do exactly as 'Doc' and I do regarding them. As sporadic fungi is the lowest order of life in the dry, so is an oyster a representative of the lowest order of animal life in water. Not only is it of the lowest order of animal life, but it is the lurking place of countless millions of the vilest of disease germs and water fungi, the sole purpose of which is to breed disease and destroy human life.

"The oyster lives upon the filthiest slime to be found on the bed of the ocean and flourishes best where the ocean currents are saturated with the sewage of cities. It feasts upon the effluvia that comes from passing ships and offal poured into the ocean by rivers. All of the slimy stuff upon which they live and fatten is thoroughly saturated with the germs of diseases of the worst kind and many fatal cases have been traced directly to the oyster.

"The oyster is a thoroughly complex organism, and possesses most of the functions of the animal body, and the microscope reveals that fact. It has intestines, heart, liver, etc., and the liver is about the largest part of it, which is a necessity due to the filthy character of its food and for the destruction of the poison it contains. Its stomach is filled with everything vile that is to be found on the bed of the ocean and, under the microscope is shown to contain thousands of disease germs of the most deadly order. If I had to eat oysters, especially raw ones, I would want my stomach to be a tank of the strongest whiskey to destroy some of those deadly germs.

"There are many other points about the oyster which I can explain if you want them, but these are enough to let you know why I don't eat oysters."

And it was enough for that crowd, half of whom were already out in the yard practicing saying "New Yawk" with their mouths open and a telephone order had been sent out for two gallons of old rye whiskey. Oysters were not on the bill of the next banquet held by that club.

WHEN THE GOAT GOT OUT.

It is twenty years or more ago that a lot of Milwaukee society people came in contact with a secret society goat, a genuine live Mr. William Goat, in full possession of his faculties to bound around and make things lively. Excelsior lodge No. 20, I. O. O. F., had a custom then of holding a dance every few weeks in the winter, which was always well attended, not only by members of the order and their families, but by their friends as well. Naturally the women had some curiosity as to the proverbial goat which the members were supposed to have ridden into the order. Among the pretty active members of the organization were Thomas Ward Taylor, now dead; Peter Van Vechten, Edward Sivyer, Thomas H. Brown, and others always as ready for a joke as I was. The women often asked Mr. Taylor to show them the goat, and he always referred them to me as the right worthy grand goat keeper. The requests came so frequently that I finally decided to show them the animal. At that time Capt. Pabst was the owner of a Billy goat. I went to him and borrowed the "critter" for the occasion one afternoon when a dance was to be given in the evening. I took the goat into a room adjoining the dance hall and decked him with red, white and blue rosetts and ribbons in fine style. I put the musicians onto the game so that when the goat would break out the music would stop short. Along about 11 o'clock when all was moving nicely and the room was a maze of dancers, I put a drop of turpentine in the goat's ear, opened the door and he went out among the dancers at a terrific gait, bounding around and bleating vociferously. "Ye-e-e-p" went the music. Women screamed. Several fainted. Others climbed upon chairs and oh, ohd. Mr. Taylor rapped with the gavel for order. Half a dozen seized the goat and hustled him back into the room. With marked solemnity Mr. Taylor assured the guests of the lodge that what they had seen had never before been revealed to any mortal outside of the membership of the order and expressed his confidence that no one of them would ever mention the fact to any person. There were numerous instances of women guests of the lodge commenting upon the enjoyableness of that occasion but none of the members ever heard of them revealing the secret of having seen the goat.

HOW I CURED A GOSSIP.

At one time there was a professional he gossip living near my beat who used to try to borrow my ear to pour gossip into very often. He would come with stories of this or that man being mixed up in affairs with women. The proceeding became tiresome and, one night I turned upon him with the old gag about the woman in Ohio who got immensely rich by attending to her own business. That cured Mr. C. and he gave me no more trouble.

A BAD, BALKY MULE.

One summer an old fellow had an electric battery on the sidewalk at the corner across Milwaukee street from the Chapman store. It was the first of the kind in town, and being a new novelty a good many persons stopped to get a shock and see how much of the current they could stand. There was usually a crowd around it and occasionally some fellow who had done some boasting got a crack that made him squirm, much to the delight of the spectators.

One afternoon an Irishman who lived out in the town of Milwaukee had been down to a Third ward vinegar factory with a big mule hitched to a dump cart with a large barrel in it, and got the barrel full of slops for his stock. Coming up the grade approaching Wisconsin street, the mule balked and positively refused all persuasion to move on. Many suggestions were offered by the crowd and tried, without effect. Finally some one suggested that the battery be turned upon him. As it was being carried into the street the mule winked the other eye and flopped his larboard ear, as if to shoo a fly from it. Some one brought a piece of wire about ten feet long, touched it to the battery and drew it along the side of that mule, the owner of the battery turning on the full current. A streak of blue flame shot along the mule's side, snapping like a bunch of fire-crackers.

That mule seemed to grow right up into the air about ten feet and with a bound he crossed Wisconsin street, the barrel of slops going out and bursting in the centre of the street, while mule and cart went north on Milwaukee street at about a 1:10 gait. The crowd yelled like a thousand bleachers at a baseball game.

GOLD COIN STOLEN.

Some years ago an insurance company placed $150 in gold coin in Bunde & Upmeyer's window to be given to school children. I told them it was not safe to leave the money there nights, but the warning was unheeded. One morning after I went off duty George Tillema saw three fellows break the window with a rock, grab the coin and skip out. They were never captured. Some people suspected the insurance company stole the money.

FINIS.

Just now, as the book is full, under the contract limit with the greatest catalogue and general job printing house in this country, a number of good items come to mind which I would like to record, but they'll have to wait until I write my next book. Here is my old key with which I registered my visits in the time clock at the Chapman store every thirty minutes during every night for thirteen years, until it was so worn it would no longer turn the register. I'll turn it here just one more last time.